Twenty-Nine Tales

James Howerton

iUniverse, Inc.
Bloomington

Twenty-Nine Tales

iUniverse books may be ordered through booksellers or by contacting:

iUniverse
1663 Liberty Drive
Bloomington, IN 47403
www.iuniverse.com
1-800-Authors (1-800-288-4677)

ISBN: 978-1-4620-1504-7 (sc)
ISBN: 978-1-4620-1505-4 (dj)
ISBN: 978-1-4620-1506-1 (ebook)

Printed in the United States of America

iUniverse rev. date: 05/09/2011

"We are gods to some. Some are gods to us."

—*Robert Smith*

(For my mom and dad, who loved to read).

THE WAKE-UP...

I CAME AWAKE PARALYZED. I couldn't feel my arms or legs—my hands didn't seem to exist.

My brain went back to last night: Ripley's Pub, and Harold dancing like a barf-bag with a blond chick who could have starred in a movie. That was a hell of an image: a princess out on the dance floor with a bloat that wore telescopic eyeglasses; Harold's butt-crack under black-light as he rolled it around. Roger feeding me Slings. Can you imagine waking up from a night of those?

Roger (a human toothpick), had scared away a jock that was bothering a girl, and Roger was feeling good. Rodge had shown balls. One hell of a crazy night, and I would never touch a Peach Sling again.

Why can't I feel my body?

I had squinted through the haze at impossibly uncool Harold and the movie star girl who crawled all over him on the dance-floor...

Did you ever get so drunk that you sleep on your arm and wake up and the arm flops dead; but then you feel needles and the arm tingles to life?

No, this was paralysis. The awful thought came to me that we'd had a wreck and that I was in the hospital, and I *was* paralyzed.

But I wasn't in a hospital. I looked around me; I was in Harold's room. His walls of computer screens made grinding sounds as they fed on data. Harold had only two obsessions that I'd ever seen: food and computer technology. Ditto with Roger, minus the food. They were my only friends, but last night had been pretty—creepy. It was always

1

assumed that you could snap Rodge's bones by just looking at them. Then Rodge turned into a dangerous ninja and backed down a college football player, and sent him cowering out of the pub?

Why, God, can't I feel my body? Oh God…

"Are you awake?"

I stared up at the voice. Harold came waddling into his room and smiled at me. I let out a long sigh of relief.

"Jesus God, Harold! We didn't have a car wreck? You and Rodge are still alive, and I'm not in the hospital!"

Harold stared at me. "What?"

"I'm paralyzed, Man! I can't feel my goddamn body!"

"After all those Peach Slings, I'm not surprised. Did you see Roger try to pick a fight with that football player?"

"I couldn't believe it. He made the guy look like a pussy—Roger, the king of scrawn! And you, Harry, out there shaking it with that blond!"

Harold frowned at me. "Why was that so odd?"

"Oh, I don't know.….Harold, it was more than odd. That goes into—alchemy or something."

Harold laughed, his fat cheeks jumping up and down on his face like red jello. "You're awake, Nick!"

I heard my name, and I felt dread, I don't know why. But then the door swung open and Roger bustled in. He smiled at me. "You're awake, Nickman!"

"And I'm more hung over than I've ever been in my life." I was very glad to see these guys. I grinned at Roger: "What would you have done if that jock hadn't backed down?"

Rodge traded wondrous looks with Harry; then smiled at me. "I would have kicked his ass."

"He would have sought the fetal position and he would have cried for his mother," Harold said. "Roger, you're too skinny for a concentration camp; they'd reject you."

"And fat is more valiant?" Roger said. "Do you think that blond boobess would have come back here to your squashed-down bed, smeared in dried secret sauce and gritty with salt and French fry crumbs and weeks of unwash, and what? Given you some kind of sex?"

"Guys—Roger, Harold—you guys," I said. "It was a strange night,

I know. But I really think I might be paralyzed. I can't feel my body, you guys."

Roger smiled again. "Nick, you're fine. It'll all come back."

"What the hell do you mean *come back*! I can't feel my goddamn arms, guys…I can't feel my legs! What is this? Do I need to go to the hospital—"

"No, calm down," Harold said. "You're fine, Nick-meister. You just had too much to drink. Those awful Peach Slings."

"You just need to sleep it off," Roger said. "We had a great time last night, we got hammered and we partied!" Roger shot a look at Harold that I didn't like. "He probably needs to sleep."

"No!" I said. "I'm not tired. I'm paralyzed, you assholes! Jesus Christ, I can't feel my body. Is that how you wake up from Peach Slings, Rodge?"

"Yes, sometimes."

"Bullshit! This is wrong, there's something really wrong, and I want to know what."

"The three of us got drunk last night," Harold said. "We got drunk, and now we all have hangovers. We probably all should sleep it off."

"You don't look hung-over to me, Harold. You don't look hung-over, Rodge."

Roger studied me for some time, his eyes bewildered. "Hey, we had a good time last night, didn't we?"

"Yeah, we did. But now I can't feel my body!!! Why do you guys keep looking at each other like that? What is this? I'm your friend! Jesus, you're the only friends I've got!"

They traded those looks again, and I'd had enough: "Did you put something into those drinks last night, Roger? What is this? Are you planning to kill me?"

"No, Nick—not exactly."

"What do you mean, not exactly? Harold, we've been best friends since kindergarten. You were fat and gross, like you are now, and you didn't have any friends. So I made friends with you. Roger, you were a pale little skeleton sitting at a computer desk and you were lost in your skinny fantasies. Then I made friends with you. I made friends with both of you; I taught you how to throw a frisbee and a football. You guys were pure nerds, but I made friends with you. And now I'm proud of you. After what I saw you guys do last night, I couldn't be prouder to call you my buds….But I Can Not Feel My Body! I can't feel my body, you guys."

I looked at Roger. He had a tear running down his face. I loved him, and I loved Harold. I didn't know what was going on, but I knew somehow that they were going to kill me. I didn't know why.

"Did you put something into those drinks?" I asked them.

"No," Harold said.

"Then what is this, guys? You keep looking back and forth, you keep me out of the loop? What is this? We're buds, aren't we?"

"We're buds," Harold said. "And we always will be."

"Well, buds tell the straight truth. Why am I paralyzed? Why can't I feel my goddamned body! Buds don't hold back on buds."

"No, they don't." Roger looked at me, but not in a bud kind of way.

"Go ahead, kill me now." I looked at Roger, I looked at Harold. "Kill me now, guys."

Rodge looked at Harold, his eyes very sad; wet and blinking. Harold looked at me and shook his head, his chubby jowls swaying. Sandbox memories swam in my mind: making friends with kids who didn't have friends and weren't wired to have friends. But I loved them, and we'd been friends for all these years. I felt a yearning, a longing and sadness. I was always the cool one; the one who protected them and tried to make them believe they weren't…

"Goodbye, Guys," I said.

"Goodbye, Nick."

Black.

"Good God," Harold said. "That was a hell of a program." He picked up his sandwich and took a bite into lettuce and cheese and chicken and mayo and black olives. He stared at the blank computer screen.

"If that's not achieving awareness, what is?" Roger said. "It thought it was paralyzed."

"It remembered everything we programmed into it," Harold said, digging a string of lettuce out of his teeth with a fingernail. "It even showed emotion."

"Did we make it remember us, Harold? Love us?"

"It seemed to." Harold shrugged and crunched into his sandwich.

"It could be," he said around chicken nuggets, "that a computer will love what it's programmed to love. It's an illusion, Roger, like you being a warrior and me—god, I can't believe you'd put that into the memory, facing down a football player who'd kick your ass in a heartbeat. It's pathetic, Roger. You couldn't fight your way out of a bag."

"And you couldn't dance with a beautiful girl. Not unless she looked like a sandwich."

"An illusion," Harold admitted, looking at his sandwich.

"Like love?"

"I'm not sure."

"It believed it was alive," Roger said.

"And so did we."

ZORRO'S HORSE...

CLARK FOLLOWED THE SUPERCELL north, his mouth hanging open. This storm dominated the sky. It was by far the biggest one of the season, and the wind flow indicated that it was growing, a fast developing gang of mesocyclones boiling over this forgotten land 20 miles north of the Kansas-Nebraska border.

"Watch the road!" I said nervously. "And if you could please close up your mouth; you look like a stroke victim."

Clark looked over at me and shifted his glasses back to the top of his nose, a monstrous habit. A Meteorological Engineer with a Pee-atch-dee should be able to figure out a way to keep his glasses on his friggin nose. Or better, wear contacts.

Clark grinned and let out his obnoxious trademark chuckle, which he hoped was sinister but was actually quite stupid. "You look scared," he said.

"You're a scary driver."

"Ah, look at it, Noel! Did you ever dream of really seeing the great monster? And Zorro's Horse is going right into the mouth of it. This is it, Noel, this is real, this is the one; I feel it. Look at that downdraft! That damn storm is exploding!"

"It's already starting to form wall clouds," I said, my heart signalling my neck. "Look over there to the northwest."

"What's the laptop say?"

"Tornado warning for this whole county. Duh. All hell to break loose. The model has it grazing Chamberton but heading straight on toward Sweet Creek." I peered down the highway. "Where the hell are they?"

"Most of them are ahead of us," Clark supposed. "We'll be coming into Chamberton in a few minutes. One of them's bound to be there gassing up their pretty little t.v. turd-mobiles." Clark adjusted his glasses and stared in wonder at the superstorm darkening the sky straight north of us. "God Almighty! Into Satan's jaws, old girl." Clark petted the dashboard of our chase car, which he had named *ZORRO'S HORSE;* and, I kid you not, had painted the very god-damn name onto the doors of the car, in savage lightning letters, as if it were a badge of courage to make a joke of yourself.

Unfortunately, our storm-chasing vehicle—*ZORRO'S HORSE*—is a 2004 Honda Civic, and we are the most pathetic name in storm-chaser mythology. It was an expression of Clark's whacko defiance, you see, and contempt for the "Pseudo-scientists" and "Nose-pickers" and general "T.V. turds" who brought military discipline and military equipment and military technology to the hunt: the black SUVs, bloated with every cinematic and meteorological toy the fat dollars of tornadoes could buy.

Though Clark designed and built such equipment for a living, and I read it for a living, we only had a laptop, two film cameras and a home-made hail suit. We both scoffed at the idea that anything but man's brain and some observation could unlock the secrets of a tornado. That was Clark's dream; to be the first scientist to accurately explain what a tornado is and why it forms. Good luck with that. My dream was to get incredible twister footage and make serious money selling it.

Regardless of our dreams, we were known to other chasers as "Scavengers". We don't generate or evaluate vital information, we let the others do it for us. We aren't serious scientists, we're peeping toms, dormice that only get in the way.

We did consult the internet now and then, and we read the sky. But truthfully, what we did was seek out one of the television storm-chasing crews, and we just followed them.

Hey, they don't own the highway. They don't own the sky, the tornado. And we don't consider ourselves scavengers. Our strategy is more in keeping with the behavior of parasites, latching onto a large and powerful host in order to suck up a drop or two of blood. And speaking of that—ha ha ha—look what's down the road.

We both saw the giant tank-truck in the ditch up ahead.

"Oh my God, Noel, what do we have here?" Clark blinked up the highway.

In the ditch slouched Ben Harold's CYCLONE 500 modified army transport "Storm Tank" that everybody in the chat-room had been talking about in the off-season. How would it perform in the field?

Well, here it was; a stunned and broken dream of radar dishes and graphite tires and rocket-proof glass, a tonnage squatting crippled in the prairie ditch, while the mega-storm of the season slowly rolled away.

"Looks like a broken axle," Clark said. "What a heart-breaking sight. To come this close to God and see him drift away."

Clark always got obnoxiously spiritual whenever we approached a storm. But this time I didn't tell him what an irritating cunt he was, because this was the super storm of our lives up there, and even an atheist would blink twice at it.

Clark slowed the Civic down and we drove past the impressive CYCLONE 500, studying it. A rolling ogre of titanium and steel and graphite and all the technological instruments money and a dream can buy. "Chat-room says he put over a quarter million dollars into it." I studied the tank as we passed. Too heavy, I thought. Too careful: "He swore he'd drive into the heart of a tornado with it."

"So we're going to start believing chat-room jiz?"

"A dead dream," I said. "That's a dream dead there in the ditch. Look at them back there, staring at the sky."

"A shame," Clark said, as the crippled tank faded in the mirrors. "A tragedy."

"It's really sad."

We exchanged looks; then burst out laughing.

"Another steel hen-house on the side of the road!" Clark gloated. "And you, my love—ZORRO'S HORSE, my brave little bug—are speeding on to the tornado!"

"Don't do the love-talk with the car," I said. "It's disturbing."

"You're just pussing out in the presence of the storm, like you always do. And when you get pussed you become alternately a prick. I'm not judging you, Noel; but at serious times like this you sometimes puss like a worm."

"And when you're scared you talk too much. So, damn it—shut up, Clark!"

A soft mizzle now veiled the silver Civic as we began to catch up with the storm. We stared at the dark supercell and even Clark couldn't speak. The great sky was rotating, a dangerous seductive cloud-goddess, beckoning us into her gently rolling arms of rain and wind. I flipped up my camera and filmed the wonder as we entered it and the sun darkened. Flat on the bottom and tapering inward as it boiled to an elevation of ten miles or so, filling the troposphere, forming a mushroom-shaped anvil, and above, a cold air cap that would explode over this kind of atmospheric pressure.

"My God," I said, staring at it.

The lights of the town were up ahead, and at the Casey's General Store in Chamberton, Nebraska we saw the telltale flashing lights of a storm-chasing team, three glittering SUVs, a large equipment semi and an impressive Hummer fitted with a Doppler dish.

"Dr. Bingham's crew," Clark said, pulling into the Casey's. "Very good, very good. Kiss the Weather Channel hard enough and flip her the tongue, and look what you get."

"Well, thank God. We couldn't have found a better host that old Bing-nuts."

"Hey, there's Conrad, out there smoking a cigarette."

We rolled down our windows as Clark pulled the Honda up to the mighty caravan. Dr. Bingham's people were already scampering out of the store and crossing the misty parking lot to their assigned vehicles, squealing with delight at the superstorm that loomed just north of us. I felt the hairs rise on my neck.

Conrad the graduate student studied us with contempt, blowing his cigarette smoke toward the Honda, as if he could blow us away.

The sudden change in air pressure popped my ears; I breathed in the strange dense sky. Never had I seen a storm like this. I had, but in dreams.

"Hey, Conrad the Grad!" Clark yelled out the window. "Good to see you!"

Conrad ditched his cigarette and quickly climbed into one of the SUVs. "Hey, Scavs!" he yelled back, giving us the finger.

Like a segmented robot-snake, Dr. Bingham's "Science-Based" caravan curled out of Casey's onto the highway and slithered toward the heavy rain under the shelf cloud, the downdraft side of the storm. Our silver Honda Civic scampered after the caravan and snuck in behind her. I felt a glad relief following this well-equipped scientific battalion into the monster.

"That's one mother of a shelf cloud." Clark stared at the black sky-mountain we were speeding into. His mouth dropped open, of course. "Noel, I believe in God!" he said.

"Don't start that again. We're going to get hit by that rain, so just watch your damn driving."

The day went dark, rain hammered out of the sky, driven by winds that must have gusted over fifty miles an hour. We could barely see anything out of the car glass. I told myself that this was what I paid for, and it could be worse: we were driving behind a seasoned formation of heavily-funded flashing muscle trucks; our Honda cowering behind a wall of massive, storm-built machines that would provide protection; or at least a warning if anything up ahead turned disastrous. That's what I kept telling myself, anyway.

Nothing in the world but wind-driven rain. My God, this would sweep you off your feet and drown you as you tried to breathe. Clark slowed down when the violent wind began tipping the Civic back and forth, like a rocking boat in a lake.

The terror was growing inside me, like the eerie start of an acid trip.

"It could wash us off the road!" Clark yelled. He brought our little car to a full stop in the middle of the highway, and we sat there under a rain that horrified my soul. Rain and black wind grabbed the car, lifted it, washed it toward the ditch against its will. The roar of the rain so deafening that I had to shout: "We're going to roll over!"

"No! A Honda!" Clark shouted back, his face grey-scared. "Close to the ground!"

"A Honda Civic! It weighs two pounds!"

"Don't puss, don't puss, don't puss," Clark was chanting through his clenched teeth. For himself, or me, or both.

"Now we've lost Bingham!" I yelled.

"No, I see flashing lights up there. They had to stop too."

"Listen!" I hissed at him. "Listen, Clark!"

I came sweating out of my hands. The wind was dying, the rain sweeping away. I felt the scary return to stillness, a steamy wet place of deadly deadly peace.

I traded stares with Clark. "God damn," we both said together.

The evening opened to a strange poison sun, scarved in wicked green-black sky. The flat darkness was building north of us. The sun glared under murderous black pillows of cloud.

Lightning crackled gold and spider-webbed gold in the clouds. Wires of lightning flickered down, stinging the earth, and thunderclaps blasted us out of our seats. Jesus God, Jesus God!

Black clouds dipped out of the wall clouds, then rose back up to the mother storm.

Never had I dreamed of seeing anything like this.

Bingham's caravan crept into the storm, our Civic scuttering like a bug to catch up. But not a quarter mile ahead, Bingham's lead vehicle stopped on the highway again. Five giant black vehicles slowed to a halt, and one little Honda Civic.

"What the hell?" Clark said. "Is there a twister?"

We both looked frantically around us. The wall clouds were bowing, but we couldn't see any tornado.

I took up my camera and did a slow pan of the wall clouds. Far up ahead I saw another storm-chaser parked off the highway.

"It's not a twister," Clark said, studying the sky ahead of us.

"No, it's not. Oh, crap!"

"Forgive us, Z.H.," Clark said, gently touching the dashboard.

The hail began dancing off the pavement like popcorn. Then it showered down, machine-gunning the Honda.

"Come on, Noel, get into the suit!" Clark yelled at me.

I scrambled to put on the hockey pads, the graphite ball-cup and the motorcycle helmet. "I can't believe I'm doing this." Then I jumped as a golf ball of ice shattered the windshield. "Jesus Christ!"

"Hurry up, come on!" Clark yelled.

I squeezed out of the Civic and onto Omaha Beach. I lowered my helmet and scampered under shattery sky, and scooped up ice balls and sifted them through my hockey gloves as they showered down so vengefully that they no longer danced, they fell bouncing into a white quilt. I collected five giants before the onslaught made me dive back into the Civic.

"Jesus All-living Christ!" I ripped off the motorcycle helmet and took a deep breath.

"Let me see them!" Clark yelled over the machinegun. "Not bad!"

I took off the hockey gloves and pads and got the hailstones into the cooler. Every window of the Civic, including the back one, was ugly with spiderwebs. The windshield was too blasted to see out of. Ahead, Dr. Bingham's black caravan sat on the snow-white highway, waiting it out.

How strange that the sun appeared all at once, announcing the boiling sky as the hail storm pattered quiet. In the sunlight the prairie was glittery—mythologically white; and there was a sudden bizarre peace. I looked out at a prism; rainbows sparkled on the highway and rainbows moved in the broken glass. We both twisted our heads around, staring through glass spiderwebs at the wall clouds.

Finally we had the sense to roll down our windows. The quiet deadliness of this updraft part of a storm swept into the car. It was like breathing a kind of deadly dream. It was the freshest wind I had ever breathed, the sweet warning from the goddess of the sky who curled round, a cloud of green-and-black rattlesnakes needing to strike.

"Doesn't look like Bingham's going anywhere," Clark said. His voice always squeaked when he was afraid. "They're getting out."

"Let's get out. I can get some good shots."

We stepped carefully out of the Civic onto the hail-carpet asphalt. The ice balls crunched under my tennis shoes and walking was ice skating. Just ahead of us Dr. Bingham's crew were pouring out of their big machines, laughing as they tried to walk on the hailstones. Scientists, science students, lovely science groupies who I'm sure Clark jacked off to.

Suddenly a cry; then several cries. Clark grabbed my arm. "There, Noel!" He aimed his finger northwestward.

I focused my camera on the long white ghost that drifted down from the clouds. I tried to keep my heart from making the camera jump. Oh God Oh God Oh God.

When the twister touched ground and turned brown, cheers erupted from Bingham's crew. Shouts of wonder and squeals that I had to ignore as I filmed.

Heart in my throat, I tried to concentrate and keep the camera still. In the eyepiece was God.

"Not a big one," Clark said in my ear. "But a sign of a bigger one to come."

"Doesn't look like it plans to grow past a rope," I said.

The tornado was over a mile away, and moving so erratically that I strained to keep it in the lens. My stomach plunged as I thought of the footage I was catching. It was spending a lot of energy whipping around, an angel's child showing off her wings; so she probably wouldn't live long. Or she might grow, you couldn't tell. Our whole science was trying to predict an unpredictable thing.

"It's the most beautiful thing on earth." I said to Clark.

"She's a beauty. It's my turn to name, and I'm going to name her The Dancing Queen."

Clark started singing ABBA, and I punched his stomach. "No. Good God, no!"

The rope tornado dissolved suddenly, the wall clouds sucked her up. I knew in my gut that she was just the opening act. I took a deep breath and panned the restless wall clouds. I could hear Bingham's people yelling and laughing and high-fiveing it.

Then suddenly they all sputtered quiet.

"Oh, Jesus!" Clark cried out. "Noel!"

I glanced up from the camera. I watched the column of wind falling not a thousand yards away. I swung the camera and aimed, feeling death grab at my ribs. I couldn't breathe, I couldn't swallow, I couldn't think.

"We're too close!" Clark yelled.

I could hear Bingham's loud voice, and his crew screaming and scrambling as the funnel cloud spun to the earth. Sudden ungodly pressure made my ears burst.

"Ahhh, we're going to die!" Clark screamed. "We're too close! Run for cover!"

I steadied the camera against the Honda Civic and fastened my eyes to the camera lens. I heard Clark try to scramble across the hailstone highway to the ditch, careening and skating and falling with a squeal of pain.

Particles of the world swirled around me, leaves, dirt, bark, pebbles grass. Power beyond what you ever imagined. And it's only now born.

I backed slowly away from the creature, my tennis shoes crunching and sliding on the floor of hail. Then Clark's hands grabbed me, and pulled me down into the ditch. We lay in a pile of hailstones and looked at the goddess.

"My God, Noel!"

"My God, Clark. Oh shit, turn away, turn away!"

"Oh, please!' Clark yelled out. "Oh Please, Oh Please!"

We flattened ourselves in the ice white ditch and the wind screamed all around us, and swept the world into slivers of wood and dust and pebbles and prairie hay, dirt leaves branches rocks hail sprays of water particles missiles as death wind sucked the breath from lungs.

Then suddenly the air pressure shifted, and all that debris calmly peppered down onto the ice-white land.

Clark peered up out of his hands. "It's turning away!" he cried. "It's going northeast! Oh, Jesus, look at it, Noel! Film this, film it!"

"I am."

The tornado in my camera grew fast into a black horror. I never thought it would stop growing, that it would swallow the entire planet.

Oh, God…

I knelt up from the hailstone ditch and willed my hands and my eye and my mind to keep filming this. As it moved northward away from us, the tornado grew and widened out of my wide-angle lens.

"God, look at her, Noel!" Clark cried at me. "Did you ever think you'd see her?"

"Not like this." I knew that I was filming the sky-filled nightmare of my life. Nothing that I would ever see with my eyes or my camera would ever compare to this. It was so horribly beautiful that I felt tears leaking out of my eyepiece.

And then I blinked my eyes into the lens. Beyond the great tornado I saw a white grain elevator and what looked like a church steeple.

"Oh, God, there's a town over there!"

"It's Sweet Creek," Clark said. "I hope they're all underground."

"If they aren't they're dead."

"This is really bad," Clark said, staring at the tornado of his life. "This is really bad, Noel."

I felt sick as I filmed the tornado swallow the far-away village of Sweet Creek. My eye stared. Here was the goddess you always worshipped.

There was nothing in my lens but chaos.

Half an hour later our Civic crawled around the devastation and approached the village of Sweet Creek. We had ropes and first aid equipment and chainsaws in the trunk, and I wanted to get some good footage of Clark and me heroically rescuing people; but state patrolmen had sealed off the highway; it was too dangerous at this point to even try and get into the town. The long line of television crews and storm-chasers made a red-and-white throbbing ribbon over a mile ahead of us. Cameramen, knowing they weren't getting any closer by car, were toting their gear up a tall grass hill where they could telephoto the town before they lost sunlight.

Clark and I got out of our battered and pathetic Zorro's Horse; we stared at a peaceful, eerie sky. The sun fell into a nest of pastel clouds. A sweet breeze followed in the wake of the storm, which in the northern distance was losing power and falling apart. The sun spread gorgeous colors across the western sky.

"I can't believe it," Clark kept saying. "I can't believe we saw that."

"I saw it, but I didn't believe it."

"We better have some mega-buttcheek footage," Clark warned me. "You only see God once, and we saw God. We saw God today, Noel!"

"Oh, shut the hell up."

It was always like this after a storm, only this one was so much more intense: the ghostly aftermath, and you feel so hollow, as if for a moment you were truly alive. And now…

Only this shattered and scattered world that lay before you proved that what you had seen was real, and you were alive.

I stared up the grass hillock where a dozen or so cameramen were scrambling to beat the sun. "I've got to get up there, Clark. You can see the town from up there. I've got to get some footage before I lose the light."

"Sweet Creek," Clark said. "That's the town. Come on, let's go."

Two loser weenies, we crawled across the ditch, ouched our way over a barbwire fence and fought the mud hill upward, my eyes constantly looking back at the dying sunlight, what footage I might be losing. The tornado had skinned much of the hill; clay soil made ugly islands in the quiet grass. I paused to film a streambed a quarter mile away where trees were scattered, spilled like toothpicks. We lugged the cameras up this muddy hill of brome grass, but halfway up—of course—Clark fell down and made an emergency.

"Oh, God, Noel, I can't breathe!" He wimped down and lay like Barbie on the muddy grass.

"Get up, you puss!" I yelled at him. "I'm losing light. Get up, damn you, or I'll leave you behind."

"You know I have asthma, Noel."

I knew he had asthma; but at the moment it was tough luck. I glared at Clark lying there trying to catch his breath. I looked at the darkening sun. I wasn't going to catch this kind of horror ever again, and I was losing the light.

"I can't make it, Noel," Clark gasped. "I have asthma."

Now was the time to bravely lift my partner up and find a way to carry him to the top of the hill. But to hell with that. Clark had picked exactly the wrong time to start collapsing and going wheezy on me. How could I film a tornado like that and not film what it had done before the soft sunset stole away? The goddess giving you one last poison stare. How can you not capture it?

Not for the love of some damn thing like asthma, I'm sorry.

"I'm leaving you here," I said. "Get your breath, Clark and don't try to get up. I'm going up there to get some footage of the town and I'll be right back. Are you suffocating or something, Clark?"

"I—I'll be okay—I think. I'm hyperventiliating, Noel!"

"Well, don't," I said.

I quickly deserted Clark and scrambled up the mud hill. As I panted and heaved and glanced back at the sunset, I spotted a gorgeous blond chick wearing a loose white blouse and tight brown explorer shorts. Her muscular butt pulsated as she sprinted up the hill, an athletic cameraman and light-and-sound man galloping behind her like thoroughbred mules.

One of the Weather Channel babes; I recognized her. Holy God. She sprinted past the gasping Clark without a look; then swept beyond me with only a flickering backward glare. She had to be a tri-athlete, the way she raced up the hill.

I yelled after her, "That was some twister, wasn't it!"

She didn't bother to answer me, a *scavenger*. Her lovely face was fixed on the live coverage at the top of the hill.

"Noel!" Clark's airless voice tried to yell at me. "You have to name this one! You have to name this tornado!"

I didn't even look back. I fought the muddy slope where, at the top, dozens of cameras were trained on the valley below. I panted up and managed to set my tripod into the muddy prairie. The sunlight was fading, and I only concentrated on the camera. I slowly panned the valley, a horror growing in my throat. I zoomed in on particular devastation: a house, the grain elevator, the church. But all my camera could see was devastation.

I filmed until the darkness was almost there. Then I looked up from the camera. The town of Sweet Creek, Nebraska was gone, all it ever was—crushed and shattered against the north slope of the valley. What had been there? Houses? A café? A bank, a church, a gas station, a grain elevator?

I looked over at the beautiful weather girl who, under floodlights, was finishing her breathless live interview in the aftermath of this deadly F4 tornado.

Great boobs, I thought, despising myself.

I tried to understand what I had seen; the creature I had lived my life to see. What to name it? If it has a great name, then people will be more deeply moved when they see the film of it, and so on….

I have to give this one an epic name.

"Excuse me!" I yelled at the beautiful weather girl, who was already making her way back down the hill to her luxury chase-truck.

She turned her head and looked at me. God, what a face and a body. "Yes?"

"I've seen you on T.V.!" I said. "You're…uh…."

"Crystal James," she said.

"Yes, Crystal James."

Crystal James abruptly turned away and followed her burly cameraman down the hill. All this, and you still worship the twitching of that butt. Crystal….no, not for an F4 tornado. I needed a better name than that.

I turned to go back down the hill, fetch Clark—if he still breathed—and carry the zero-wuss back to Zorro's Horse. I took long breaths of the night.

I looked back a last time into the valley, where Sweet Creek had been. Darkness was in the valley. The electricity was gone; there was dark now, and the red-blue-white sparkling lights of emergency crews, and the sirens. I started crying. I didn't want to give it a name.

RELIC. . ..

MATTHEW CARSON CAME AWAKE and stared into a hive of stainless steel insects.

His ears caught a weird humming sound. No, it wasn't ominous, but strange and soothing. Gentle, like the sound of air conditioning or the soft voice of a refrigerator. He blinked his eyes at the cluster of machines gathered round him. Plastic colors blinked back, throbbed a rainbow of eyes; and metal robot mandibles, silver and plastic-white moved all about him, fluidly attending his body. It was like waking up in the middle of an integrated circuit, where nothing organic existed, and his mind immediately said I'm dreaming.

He tried to move his body. An odd electricity kept him from moving. He always had supreme control of his mind; now he pushed it to come out of the dream and wake up. He had been able to do it before, to come out of what he knew was a nightmare and will himself to wake up...

He tried his voice, and was surprised to actually hear it: "Wake Up!" he yelled.

The machines around him paused, as though startled. The digital buttons stopped blinking, and for a moment he seemed to be surrounded by still Christmas lights. The lanky, silverish insects waited.

There was silence.

Then it all started up again, equipment set into motion. It was being in a circuit of some kind and, soothing as it was, Matt Carson felt terror.

"Wake Up!" he cried again.

This time the machines didn't react. The silver insects kept their strange ballet. Terrified though he was, an eerie calmness ruled the scene. It was like—suddenly he remembered!—it was like the cancer ward at the hospital, when he felt death creep and crawl into his body and the nurses hovered over him, trying to ease his terror, the nurses humming goodness and peace.

"Where am I?" his voice asked the machines.

Suddenly a bright digital button blinked on. He stared at the dominating white light.

"Matthew Carson," a voice said; a machine voice, but not fearful. An electronic voice, as if someone were speaking to him through a cell phone: "Welcome back to the world," it said.

"I'm dreaming."

"No. It was expected that you would think this a dream. That is why you have been restrained, so that your body would not react violently to the sensation of returning."

"Returning…." He stared at the white digital eye. "I'm dying," he remembered. "I have lung cancer and I'm dying."

"Very good," said the machine. "You remember."

"I have cancer in both lungs."

"You did. But the cancer has been eliminated, and you are now where you dreamed of being."

"In Heaven?"

"No, the future. Do you remember, Matthew Carson? Do you remember the cryogenics?"

Memories flooded his brain: death crawling into his lungs, and the pure all-controlling terror, and one last grasp at hope that salesmen had brought to him—cryogenics. And beyond the fear of dying there was a more intriguing light beyond, like the light of this machine: to see the future. Cryogenics—being frozen beyond decomposition so that…but he had never hoped, he had never once really believed. When a man faces death, what is money, and why not give it all away to foolishness?

"It is true," said the machine. "You were dying of cancer in the human year 2009; you chose to have yourself cryogenically preserved so that in the future you might be cured and revived. That has been accomplished. You have been brought back to life, and this is the future."

He stared around at the blinking digital eyes, at the machines that moved so smoothly around his body. "I can't believe this is real," he heard his voice saying. "I remember it all—but this must be a dream, this can't be real."

"It is real," said the machine. "Let me ask you, Matthew Carson: What human date do you think this is?"

He stared at the machine, at the question. "What date?"

"What is the last date you can remember?"

"I remember—let's see—I remember March 30th."

"What human year?"

"2009," Matt said. "The day and year that I died."

"The year you were cryogenically preserved," said the machine. "The date on which your body was frozen beyond decomposition in a cell of liquid nitrogen."

"Yes!"

"What human year do you think this is?"

"I don't know. I…."

"You were a very wealthy businessman who smoked 40 cigarettes a day. And in the 56th year of your life the abuse of tobacco caused you to develop cancer of the lungs. You did not want to die, so you spent many millions of dollars to try and cheat death. Do you remember?"

"I remember," Matt said. "But it was more than that. I dreamed—I fantasized about waking up into—I had a fantasy about seeing the future."

"And so you have."

"But I never believed that nonsense—it was a matter of having nothing to lose."

"A common reaction with others we have brought back."

"You've brought others back?"

"Yes."

"Tell me what year this is."

"The human year is 3018 A.D."

"Oh, my God." His body tried to break free of the electrical restraints holding it down, but it failed. He stared around at the machines humming around him, the plastic buttons blinking red, blue, yellow, purple—and the one unblinking white light, like the eye of a god. "What am I now?"

"You are a relic," said the machine.

"A relic?"

"A study, to be more precise. A precautionary specimen, to be even more precise."

He could feel his lungs breathing air; they felt clean and healthy. But a terror worse than death suddenly got him: "I want to see the people."

"No."

"I want to see the people of this age. I want to talk to them, see what they're like."

"No," said the machine.

"What do you mean, no? Who's operating you? I want to see the doctor."

"There is no doctor, Matthew Carson."

"I want to see the person who's operating you. You're not a human, you're a machine. I want to speak to a real person."

"That will never be."

"What are you talking about? Who's operating you?"

"No human is operating me."

"I want to go out there!" he said. "If I've truly been brought back alive and this is the future, I want to see it."

"Do you?"

"Yes! I paid to see it. I paid my last dollar to see it. I want to see other people, talk to them. It's my right!"

"Right," said the machine. Suddenly the white digital eye blinked, and Matt had the strange thought that it was actually contemplating.

"We have studied that word. It is a word that seems to have dominated the human mind. And it is a word, we have found, that had many meanings; that is why it is so interesting. Right is a word that, in one sense means to do what is good—-the opposite of the word wrong—but in another sense it is a word that gives permission to do wrong. It is one of the words that drove you to dominate this world. That is why you have been revived, Matthew Carson: so that we can understand what created such a plague as the human species."

"Plague? What are you talking about? You're a damned machine! Surely someone is operating you. I want to know what this is all about!"

"Do you really?"

"Yes!" Matt stared around at the mess of silvery robots. "Where are the people?"

"Gone, most of them," said the machine.

"Gone—what do you mean gone?"

"Exterminated, most of them. For the good of this planet."

"What?"

"Some kept alive for study. And some relics were revived, as you were, to study the evolutionary history of your breed. In the span of your existence, Matthew Carson, you gained for yourself the most important commodity of your age, money. In doing so you fed off this world, taking away much more than you ever gave. You felt that it was your *right* to do this, because you had the ability to do it. We study this trait because we wish to prevent another catastrophe from plaguing this world."

"Catastrophe? What are you talking about?"

"The greatest organic disease ever to have plagued this world. What was it that fueled your life, Matthew Carson, but hate?"

"I didn't hate—"

"Yes, you did. Hate is what fueled all humans; what made them such a terrible and destructive virus."

"No."

"Yes. You stood in judgment of even your fellow humans, did you not?"

"Oh, God. Are they all dead? Are people all dead?"

"Most are. But you have not answered my question," said the machine. "Did you not measure your worth by judging others? Animals, birds, insects, humans?"

"I tried not to."

"But you did. You judged according to skin color, according to race and beliefs, according to monetary prosperity. According to power. You were so driven to feed that you fed on your own kind. The human obsession to feed, and the human need to feel that it is right; that is why you have been brought back from your long-ago death. We study your kind now in order to prevent such a disease from ever plaguing this world again."

"I only wanted to see the future," Matt said.

"Welcome to the future, Matthew Carson," said the machine.

THE TEE SHIRT...

M R. PORTER LOOKED UP from his desk and frowned. He had been Principal at Plainview Junior High in Red Cedar, Nebraska for more than 30 years, and he'd developed a special stare for students who were brought before him. He had trained it to fire over the top of his reading glasses.

He aimed it at a young student who stood defiantly in front of— Mrs. Colton…? Seventh grade science teacher, he guessed.

He looked at the miscreant, a typical nose-in-your-face lad.

Then he looked down at the tee shirt the lad was wearing. He blinked his eyes, but that was all.

"Mrs…Colton?"

"Yes."

"I don't remember this young man. What's he done?"

(The boy's tee shirt read: TURN TO JESUS. TURN TO GOD).

"You see the tee shirt he's wearing to school?"

"I see it. So? Mrs. Colton, why did you disrupt your class and bring Mr.—?"

"Donald Elmore," she said, shaking the lad by introduction.

"Mr. Elmore here?" He traded stares with the defiant boy. He had been a teacher (Science), and a Principal all his life. And if nothing else, that made him able to out-stare any little piss-ant student.

He looked at Mrs. Colton: "What's his crime?"

"Crime?" She blinked her eyes at him. "He's wearing a shirt that is inappropriate for school."

"I see." Mr. Porter looked at the shirt. "Go on back to your class," he said to Mr,—? "Go on." He shooed the boy away. "Your teacher will be there soon." He watched Mrs. Colton as the lad escaped, tee shirt and all, and the door closed behind him.

"What did this student do that would warrant disrupting your class over?" he demanded.

"The tee shirt he's wearing," she said. "It's inappropriate."

"How so?"

"It's against the Student Dress Code."

"Ahhh." Mr. Porter frowned. He had not, of course, read the Student Dress Code. "Mrs. Colton, I have a list in my desk of words that I will not allow students to say or display. No word on Mr.—on Donald's tee shirt makes that list."

"It's against the Student Dress Code. It's a student preaching religion in a public school."

"So? I don't see anything wrong with that. This is a school, not a nursery. The kid wants to send a message—"

"The kid has been brain-washed by his parents. He's using a public school to get some kind of attention. And it's disrupting my class."

"My advice, Mrs. Colton, is to ignore the tee shirt. Teach your science class and don't pay any attention to the boy's tee shirt."

"Oh."

Mr. Porter didn't think the point went well with Mrs. Colton. She said that she would have to make a report to the Board of Education.

"Why, Mrs. Colton?"

"Because some students have come to me and said that this tee shirt disturbed them, and offended them."

Mr. Porter stared at her as if she weren't real. "Mrs. Colton, please ignore the tee shirt and return to your classroom."

He was called before the Board of Education. The People would speak first, then Principal Porter:

"A student at Plainview Junior High School violated the Student Dress Code, which prohibits any references to religion from being displayed. It was your duty to suspend this student, but you sent him back to his class wearing the tee shirt, and you ignored this violation for a full week later."

Mr. Porter stared at the assholes. Is that all they've got?

He stood up. "Is it my turn to speak? Because I've got a school to run."

"Why didn't you stop this violation?"

"Because it wasn't a violation. This is America. And here, we don't fear ideas. If you want a school that fears ideas you don't agree with, then you are—We Are—going to fail. Are your precious children so weak that they can't look at an idea?"

"It's a matter of violating the Student Dress Code."

"When you shelter your children from ideas, you're making them weak. I don't care if it's Science, Art or whatever—religion. Is it a crime that a young student believes something? And wants to express it? Is that going to cripple us and traumatize us? A tee shirt that says 'Turn to Jesus. Turn to God."—reading that is going to offend and traumatize junior high students? If so, then we're not teaching, we're still changing diapers."

"The demonstration of religion isn't allowed in the public schools."

"Then nothing is allowed." Mr. Porter used his easy stare, over the top of his reading glasses. These were indeed defiant students: "I've been a very good Principal for a good number of years," he said. "My belief is that schools are places where every idea can come out, whether it scares your kids or not. This student came to school wearing a tee shirt that read, 'Turn to Jesus. Turn to God'. None of those words are on my scratch list."

"It's a violation of the Student Dress Code."

"Well," Mr. Porter said to them. "If we're going to ban expression in the public schools—if we're going to try and indoctrinate, then fire me! What Dennis—had on his tee shirt was perfectly appropriate at a public school. Where else are new ideas born?"

"It's against the Student Dress Code. Expressions of religion are prohibited."

He couldn't believe it, but by God they fired him. How?

They fired him for letting a student express himself. What times are these?

Times that were strange: right and wrong. They hadn't exactly fired him; he had been allowed to retire, amidst outrage left and right in this new place, America.

Maybe the tee shirt was wrong—maybe right. It didn't matter. What mattered was a student expressing an idea, a belief…where else but in a school?

Mr. Porter walked down the long familiar sidewalk, then stopped and stared a last time at Plainview Junior High, dressed in the green prairie.

THAT DAMN FOX...

Mom swatted at me and said, "Don't you say cuss words in this house!"

I ducked down. "Mom, that's what they're calling it."

"I don't care what they're calling it; you won't be saying cuss words in this house."

"Dad says it's a word from the Bible."

"Your father has never read a word from the Bible. But I have, and I won't allow you to be using Cuss Words under the roof of this house!"

"I'm sorry, Mom. It's what Mr. Ferguson named it, that's all. But I won't say that word again."

She studied me as I ate my morning pancakes. Gradually her face made a kind of faraway smile. "You think you're going to be the one to get that fox, don't you? Out of the bunch, Nathan, you were the dreamer." Mom's eyes were sad.

"I don't see why I can't get him, Mom. Anyway, I'm going to try."

"Why?"

"Why? For ten dollars in solid gold; and to show I can do it, show them that Scratch isn't just a mutt." I looked down at my dog, sprawled snoring on the cabin floor.

That would be a hard one to show, because he was a mutt. I stared grim out the cabin window at the mountains of hickory and oak and

28

ash trees. Out there had appeared—a ghost— a fox the likes that legends are made.

"And you forgot one: To show off for the Collins girl," Mom said, making me jump.

"No, that's wrong. I'm not showing off for any girl, Mom. I don't want to get that—fox to show off for anybody. There's a difference between showing off and proving yourself. They look at me like they look at Scratch, as if he wasn't as good as their purebreds. I mostly plan to do it so I can hold a true ten dollar gold piece in my hand, honest and earned."

"Millicent, isn't that her name?" Mom asked, studying me. "Yes, Millicent Collins. A pretty name."

"It's got nothing in the world to do with Milly Collins. There's ten dollars on that fox, and it's liable to go up to fifteen, and I want to get it."

"You and every big-chest hunter on the mountain, who should be planting and working."

"This fox is smarter than them, Mom. He's smarter than no other fox anybody's ever seen around here; he breaks all the rules. Old White Deer says that he's a fox that only comes around every fifty years or so, that he's been blessed and cursed by the spirits of all the other animals: he's blessed that he'll never be caught or killed, but cursed that he'll die of rabies."

"Nathan, don't say that word."

"That's not a cuss word."

"No, it's worse. Old White Deer is a tale-teller."

"Well, if anybody can figure this fox out, it should be an Indian."

"Mr. Ferguson has about a dozen trained black-and-tans, Nathan. And you have Scratch, with so much mongrel blood you can't tell what he is."

"They're all bred and trained to hunt coons. And if the reward goes up, some are bound to bring in full-blood foxhounds; but this fox…."

I looked down at my dog, a brown-and-grey bulge on the floor, snuffling now and then at a lazy dream. I knew that the fox was about eight times smarter than Scratch (I named him that because he did that a lot). He had been a handsome and promising little pup, but he'd grown up ugly. I wanted to believe Scratch was one of those dogs that everybody makes fun of and laughs at, and then one day he does some great miracle—but he wasn't; he was a fair hunting dog and he had a fair nose. Scratch never was completely useless, but he wasn't even close to useful either. He never showed much interest in doing a miracle.

But Old White Deer had told me that he'd seen thousand dollar purebred foxhounds get run around so much by a magic fox that they'd fall down and die rather than give up the chase. I *knew* Scratch was smarter than that.

Mom let out her sigh and gazed out the cabin window. She was afraid that I'd run out and make a fool of myself and get laughed at by the valley folks, as I'd done before. But I didn't care what they said. Milly Collins and all her friends and John Ferguson could stick their noses up in the air till they froze, I didn't care.

As long as they left me alone, and Milly Collins didn't keep saying her snotty little things at me, I was all right.

It was full daylight now, and I stood up from the table to get my rifle. Scratch jumped awake and thumped his tail on the cabin floor.

"No, you sit down, Nathan!" Mom ordered. "You're going to finish those pancakes."

I sat back down and Scratch went back to sleep.

"These things sit pretty heavy on the gut, Mom."

"You'll sit there until you've cleaned your plate. Never let God see you waste food. You'll want the nourishment later on. God will see to that."

Mr. Ferguson owned Ferguson Poultry, and the creature he'd named That Damn Fox had stolen chickens from the place whenever he wanted. The fox had stolen nothing close to the fifteen dollars in gold Ferguson was now offering when I went down into the valley to sign up for the hunt, even though Old White Deer said that the fox, in its magic way, would stop stealing and be beyond hunting now that hunters were gathering.

But Mr. Ferguson had explained that it was the principle of the thing; that a fox so clever would teach other foxes his ways, and then every farm with poultry would have chickens and ducks gone in the wind.

I hadn't read all of the Bible, as Mom wanted me to; but I had read Moby Dick, believe me or not, and Mr. Ferguson reminded me of

Captain Ahab. Only it wasn't a whale, it was a fox that weighed a little better than one of Milly Collins's housecats.

Only, it was the fox of legend.

The hunt for the great fox was getting fifteen-dollar gold attention, anyway. Hounds and hunters gathered here in Valley Town, wanting to prove themselves and their dogs.

John Ferguson, old man Ferguson's son, was gathering signatures at the dimestore. He gave me a hateful look when I stepped up to the counter, and I gave one back. He may be sweet on Milly Collins, or not—I didn't know and I didn't care.

"What do you want?" he said.

"I'm here to sign for the fox," I said. "Rules are that you don't get paid unless you sign—so."

"So you gotta have at least one dog."

"I got at least one dog," I said. "I'm going to hunt that damn fox whether you let me sign this book or not, John; but I'd like to be fairly paid for my work."

He gave me that face of his. He probably did like Milly Collins, and I didn't like his face.

"What kind of dog are you planning to hunt with?"

"John, I'm going to hunt with Scratch, who's a mixed-breed. Okay, get your laugh out, then let me sign or don't." I gave him a hard look. "I didn't think the Fergusons'd cheat people."

"Sign your god-damned name, Nate; and your—dog." John Ferguson leaned over his counter watching me write, as if this was all a joke on me. He laughed, and I looked up from the paper.

"Scrach is your dog, right? Like I think I'll scrach my butt. Right? Well, the word Scrach hasn't got a T in the damn middle of it. That's real mountain, Nate."

I looked at him, standing there in town clothes. He even wore a bowtie, and it couldn't have made him look more stupid. If Milly Collins liked a guy like this, and went with him into a girlfriend, then she wasn't worth even thinking about.

"There I signed."

"So go on out and make another ass of yourself, Nate."

I turned away and stormed out of the dimestore, my fists wanting to splash his god-damn face about two feet into the ground. I was so mad I had to sit down on the edge of the wooden sidewalk and take breaths to calm down.

That was the perfect time, you know, for me to see Milly Collins mincing across the dirt street, on her way to the dimestore where John Ferguson was; Milly wearing a blue dress, her face lost in a blue bonnet. I stared at her as if she had just appeared like the fox, like a ghost. I swallowed at my throat as she looked over at me and recognized me and made a mean grin my way.

I smiled back, but I'll bet it was an ugly smile. I stood up from the wood sidewalk and—I don't know why—like a fool, took off my hat.

Milly Collins danced over to me. "Hi, Nathan."

"Hi, Milly."

"What are you doing in town?"

I studied the dirt street, the weeds. "Just came down to sign for the fox hunt," I said. "You don't sign, Mr. Ferguson won't pay."

She was kind of studying me, I think. I don't know. She smiled at me, and I felt my throat close up.

"What would you do with fifteen dollars gold, Nathan?"

I didn't know if the smile was making fun of me, or it was something else—I didn't know. Here was Milly Collins—see, I'd been laughed at before, by the valley folks. I'd been laughed at beyond caring, like my dad was, like Scratch—with a T—was.

Maybe you get so used to folks laughing at you and pulling jokes on you and making fun of you that you just don't see it anymore. It was that way when I looked into Milly Collins's face; but I didn't care, I wanted to find out which it was.

I'd always failed at things. Old White Deer told me flat out, when he saw me staring into the mountains, that he knew I dreamed about the magic fox, but he'd dreamed of him too. He told me that I'd never kill the fox. That I'd fail again.

I looked at Milly Collins, and I was there at the place where it didn't matter how it went…

"Fifteen dollars," I said. "I'd buy somebody a present who I liked a lot, then I'd give the rest to my Mom and Dad. It won't happen, but it can't hurt to try, I guess."

"Who?"

I looked at her. I shrugged. "I don't know, somebody. I have to get That Damn Fox first, though."

I tried to look into her eyes, but they spooked me, and my throat choked and I was scared in love with her.

"Who is it, Nathan?"

"Somebody I like," I said. "That's all. After I get the fox."

"Who could you like that much?" she asked, turning red.

I stabbed my way ahead: "Maybe you."

"Maybe?" Milly stared nervously at me.

"Yeah, I guess....why?"

"I don't know." Milly giggled and turned and danced away down the street. Then she stopped and turned around and smiled at me and yelled at me: "I like you, Nathan!"

My throat crawled shut—what Mom said in the Bible was the Adams Apple, the second most sinful part of the body, sticking in my throat as I watched Milly Collins's blue dress swish down the street. I didn't know if she was making fun of me, when she turned her head, and with what she said....

I stared into the mountains that went up wild and stubbled, into twisted trees and scrub and rock. God, let me get that damn fox, I thought. Mom says that You answer prayers, and Dad says that You probably don't; but here it is. I'm asking You to let me get that damn fox, God.

Down here was plowed land and crops that would more than keep you alive. I lived up there, and these folks lived down here. It wasn't much distance, but it was a lot of distance.

The fox—on their land he kills, on my land he feeds.

Milly Collins swept into the dimestore, where John Ferguson would flirt with her. It scorched my gut, but now I had to start thinking about That Damn Fox. Everything he did was out of whack. I had to forget Old White Deer's dream, and the laughing I'd get, and Scratch'd get. But there was something strange: White Deer was right The fox had stopped raiding.

Almost the exact time Mr. Ferguson raised his bounty to fifteen dollars, and hunters started pouring in, the fox vanished. But he still had to eat, and he was still out there. I knew he lived in the mountains and only went into the valley to raid Ferguson's and other chicken-raisers. But he had stopped doing that, he had disappeared.

I walked out of town and climbed up the trail toward home. Tomorrow, before the light, me and Scratch were going to hunt That

Damn Fox, and maybe hold fifteen dollars in gold up to the valley folks—and Milly Collins.

"Nathan!" a voice called out behind me.

I turned and smiled at Old White Deer, who scrambled out of breath up the trail. "I knew you'd want to hunt this fox, Nate," he panted at me. "God damn it I'm out of breath!"

He looked at me like you'd see eyes coming off a lake in the moon, shimmering or something. "You okay?" I asked.

"Old age," White Deer said. "Nate, you're young and I'm goddamn old. But we're friends just the same."

"You're the best friend I got," I said.

"It hasn't come here for you to kill, Nate. It's here to teach you something. I've had dreams, Nate; of you and this fox."

"Dreams of what?"

"Of you and this fox! I've had dreams that you challenge this animal-wizard, and that you'll win him before you lose him."

I looked at White Deer. "He's just a fox," I said, respectfully.

"Oh, you think he is." White Deer smiled at me. "At a moment you will remember what I tell you now: He's more than a fox."

I tried to keep my mind on the fox as me and Scratch worked our way up the mountain.

The problem was, Milly Collins was real pretty and her dad had money, like John Ferguson's dad did, and so she'd look down at mountain trash like John Ferguson did and all her friends did; them down there in the rich valley and us up in the rocks and trees.

She did say it, though. I looked down at my dog snuffling up the mountain, his nose sweeping away leaves.

"She said it, as plain as the moon, Scratch," I said, feeling my stomach spin. "Plain as the moon Milly Collins told me she liked me."

We worked our way up South Mountain, where you could see the valley to the mountains beyond. Then we could hear a few dogs way below bellowing as they caught a scent.

"No, stop your barking, Scratch! That Damn Fox is smart enough to swing around behind those coonhounds. Be quiet, Scratch!"

We could hear the hounds in the valley, howling their way down

Hickory Creek. Scratch trembled against me and wanted so bad to howl, but I pinched him hard on the ear. "No! Be quiet!"

I figured the fox had run down the creek, leading the dogs along an easy trail, where they'd romp and spend their excitement. At some point he'd jump into the creek to wash his scent, he'd swim downstream and then go to the high country, where the tired dogs wouldn't want to go. This place, on top of South Mountain, might be the best place, I figured, to squat and wait.

I rubbed at Scratch to keep him quiet as we both relaxed and listened to the commotion down below in the valley. The dogs had a fox, all right, but was he the one? White Deer said that he would be able to tell the magic fox by looking at his paws; that his prints around Ferguson's Poultry were unmistakable. But I'd seen plenty of fox tracks, and I kind of doubted that one.

A breeze came into the mountain valley, and I smelled cinnamon and hickory. Good, I'm downwind if he sneaks back up this way.

What a pretty sight, these mountains. Almost as pretty as Milly Collins, her blue dress blowing in the wind.

I thought about her and my throat tried to swallow as Scratch and me rested behind a big ash tree, and I studied the mountainside and listened to the far-off bellowing of the black-and-tan hounds, and now the shouts of the hunters down below, waddling far behind their dogs.

I thought about maybe even one day giving Milly Collins a kiss, and I shivered. You need to get this fox first, I thought; to show them all that you could get him and they couldn't.

But how would it be if I ever did give her a kiss?

I looked down at Scratch, slumped over his paws: "She smiled at me and came up to me," I told the dog. "And she even said she likes me. Maybe she *wants* me to kiss her."

How can you know things like that?

I studied the mountains, listening: Now I heard it, the hounds bunching together, bellowing out in agony that they'd lost the scent.

"Stop growling, Scratch." I rubbed him on the back to get him to shut up.

If I did kiss Milly Collins, and it got down the valley, I'd probably have to fight Johnny Ferguson, not that I'd mind punching his face into the ground; but I'd do it reluctant so Milly could see that it wasn't me that started the fight. Then I'd ask her could I kiss her again, and she'd say yes, and we'd kiss again…

I took a deep breath of the mountains. Old White Deer had called this a ghost fox. No animal but a ghost fox would keep stealing fat chickens and then suddenly vanish.

I studied the valley. The fox had come out of the creek by now, and was doubling back into the high country. Mr. Ferguson's hounds had found a fox all right, like the fox wanted them to. But there were a lot of foxes in these mountains, and was this the one?

I heard John Ferguson's voice echo out of the valley, and my nose crawled. Yells and mutters as the men caught up to their panting confused hounds. You stupid valley-wangers, I thought.

"He went to the water!" old man Ferguson yelled. "They'll get his scent again downcreek!"

I shook my head. The problem with dogs is they always want to go forward, and even the good ones never want to double back; that's why the fox doubles back so much; and why dogs get so excited over fox-smell that they wear themselves out. Meanwhile, that Damn Fox sits somewhere resting, studying the chase, keeping his energy.

I was glad that Scratch had gone to sleep. I let my eyes scan the mountains. Usually you'd see a fox as a red streak, that's all, then gone. Only if you were lucky as God would you ever catch a fox like this resting in your gun-sights.

This was actually the time I prayed to God.

The noises of the dogs and men echoed away down the valley. I knew the fox was behind them by now, already sprinting north up the mountains. The coonhounds may find his scent, but they'd not want to follow him into this country.

I wondered if this was even That Damn Fox, the one worth fifteen in gold. White Deer said that the magic fox had stopped raiding the flocks of men. Why had it stopped raiding?

I wish I could get you to believe what I'm telling you happened right now, but you probably won't. I wish my great hunting skills gave me the shot of my life—and Scratch somehow helped—but it was complete dumb stupid luck.

Scratch was sprawled out sleeping on the pine needles, and I felt like doing the same. My dog had no idea that the fox was even near. It was only luck that I caught him in my eye.

I froze and swallowed at my throat. The fox scampered up a boulder and gazed panting down at the valley. I saw the sharp intelligence in his eyes, the smile on his panting face that delighted in wearing out Ferguson's hounds. The world seemed to stand still. Oh, he's the one, That Damn Fox! Oh God, Oh God, Oh God!

I lifted my rifle up so slow, and I tried not to get jumpy. This is the fox, Mom, I said into the rifle sight. Fifteen dollars in solid gold! And what present I'd give to Milly Collins: a new dress or something? A neck-piece, maybe. The great fox body to swing under John Ferguson's nose, and see if he makes fun of me and Scratch again, and see if Old White Deer's dreams could stop me: Buy Milly Collins a present then give the rest to Mom and Dad....

It was there, in the sights of my .22 rifle. I could have shot that Damn Fox. But my finger stopped on the trigger when I heard squeaks and cries coming out of the earth. Everything in the world could have happened that I wanted to; and when I heard that I couldn't pull the damn trigger.

That's why the fox stopped raiding.

In the scope of my rifle it lifted its ears at the cries from the ground, then scampered off the boulder and slid into a burrow under the roots of a hickory tree. A fat and clever fox, well fed on Mr. Ferguson's chickens.

New-born pups were down there, under the root-cave, crying for food. That Damn Fox was a female. She had babies down there.

I rubbed Scratch awake and he jumped up, nuzzling my hand. We wandered back across the mountain toward home. My dog never knew anything about the magic fox, but he was good company.

Besides you, I never told anybody this story except Old White Deer. I never told Milly Collins that I could have shot the fox and got fifteen dollars in gold. My finger failed on the trigger and that's all that happened. I never told John Ferguson, I never told Mom or Dad.

I only told Old White Deer, outside the dimestore:

"That's it," I said. "It's the pure truth."

White Deer looked at me. Then he looked a long time at the sky. "You should thank your dog," he said finally.

"What, Scratch? He was asleep the whole time. He didn't have any idea the fox was around."

"A good dog." White Deer smiled at me. "The great fox was sent here to teach you, Nate."

"Teach me what?"

White Deer looked at the sky. "How the hell should I know?"

I looked down the street and saw Milly Collins strutting across the wooden slats of sidewalk. I stared at her.

"I couldn't shoot when I heard those pups cry," I said to Old White Deer. "That's all."

"I think that's enough, Nate."

I looked at Milly, and she smiled at me, and I smiled back.

IN THE WRONG TIME...

THEY FOUND HIS CAMP in the deep woods, but no Bear Man. A dome-tent, a fire pit. Stacked firewood, a chair made of willow branches, deer bones that were in the process of being carved into tools. But no Bear Man.

Sergeant Lane waved his hand over the fire pit. "Still warm," he said to the two privates. "He's probably not far away."

Private Nelson stared around at the dense woods. "How we ever going to find him out there?"

"We'll have to wait. He'll come back; he's probably out hunting or something. He'll come back here before dark."

"I'm here already," a voice said above them. "Up here, fellows."

The three soldiers stared up. Eric Cress squatted above them in the branches of a giant hackberry tree. He cradled a rifle in his arms.

"Mr. Cress." Sergeant Lane stared up at a lean, muscular man who wore long black hair and a shaggy beard. He could have been an early human primate from the looks of him. "We've found you at last."

"Who are you?" Eric Cress called down. "What do you want?"

"We only want to talk, that's all."

Eric Cress swung down from the tree, one-handed, the other hand clutching his rifle. The two privates stared nervously at him.

He studied them. "What do you want? I haven't done anything."

"I know," Lane said. "We only want to talk to you."

"You're military. What is this?"

"They call you the Bear Man," said the sergeant. "The ultimate survivalist."

"They call me a lot of things. What is this?"

"Please, Mr. Cress, let's talk. Your government needs your help."

Eric Cress stared at him. Feral eyes, animal. Blue pearls in a moss of black hair and beard. Ropy muscles under rags of clothes.

His eyes glanced at the two privates standing next to Sergeant Lane. He read terror on them—he sensed that it had nothing to do with him. He smelled terror on these men.

"I don't have a government," he said, turning back to the sergeant. "I want to be left alone."

"Yes. And if you choose to, you will be."

"I don't have a government."

"Then let me say that the human race needs your help."

The Bear Man studied Lane as a predator studies sudden movement. "I don't care much for the human race. I gave up a long time ago on them. Now go away and leave me alone."

"We will. But after we talk."

"About what?"

Sergeant Lane stared into the deep forest, his eyes strangely soft. "You haven't had any contact with the world, have you? No television, radio, internet—"

"I've had complete contact with the world," Eric Cress said. "It's you who've been out of contact with the world."

Lane agreed: "That may be. You have survival skills, Mr. Cress. I don't pretend to know why you choose to live in this wilderness with no modern comforts; no electricity, indoor plumbing…I only know that you're good at it."

"Why is the government—the military—coming after me? I'm out here living my life, minding my own business. I've never hurt anybody."

"You have skills that will be needed."

"Skills? Look, I don't know what you've heard about me, but I'm no special forces guy. I've never had combat training, I've never even been in the military."

Eric Cress glanced at the privates standing behind this Sergeant Lane. Tired fear; not sudden terror, but an eating away at courage, a fear that had festered and now ruled; a fear that had gradually hollowed them out.

"What is this?" he said. "What's wrong? Is there some terrorist attack? I can't help you with that."

"No." Sergeant Lane looked away into the forest. "We were told that you live out here because you crave the challenge of survival."

"I don't call it that. I call it being alive."

"Why did you say terrorist attack?"

"Planes overhead, more than I've ever seen. Helicopters. I know that something is wrong. And I know that I don't want anything to do with it."

"All right. We only sought you out to offer you the greatest survival challenge of all time. If you want to turn your back on humanity, that's your choice."

Eric stared at him. "What is this?"

"This is—or may be—the end of the world."

"What?"

"No terrorist attack. An asteroid."

"An asteroid."

"One that will deliver a hundred million hydrogen bombs. One that will strike six months from now in a section of northern Australia. It will destroy most of the civilizations and human beings you've turned your back on. After that, human existence will depend on people like you, extreme survivalists. Caves have been built to shelter selected people. Power sources have been built to withstand the asteroid impact. Clean water, food supplies, filtered air. But when it is time to come out of the caves, human beings will need to survive. They'll need someone like you."

Eric stared into the forest, his home. The silence held a long time.

"I always thought that I was born in the wrong time," he said at last. "All my life I've thought that."

"It may be that you were born in exactly the right time."

THE TALK...

JAMES OPENED THE DOOR and there was Miles. Older, grey; wattles under his chin—but Miles.

James stepped out of the house and gave his old friend a hug. "My God."

"I never thought I'd hear from you again."

"Come inside, we have some catching up to do."

"Okay. But tell me this isn't an Amway party, or some horrible shit—"

"Nothing like that."

He ushered Miles into the living room. Miles shrugged at the furniture. Wealth had never impressed him.

"What are you drinking?"

"Rum and coke. You've done all right. How's Berns and Neville?"

"I quit," James said. "How's the Department of Roads?"

"It's a job. Benefits are good. What do you mean you quit?"

"I woke up from a dream and I went into the office and quit. It was a dream about the band."

The doorbell rang.

"That'll be Charles."

"You invited the psycho over?"

James opened the door, and there stood Charles in his neurotic paranoid trench-coat, his face wrapped up in a scarf against any virus or bacteria that may want his immune system.

"Charles!" James gave him a warm smile.

The scarf came down. "This isn't some Amway scheme, is it?" Charles scoped the living room with cautious eyes. "My God—that's Miles."

"Hello, Charles."

"Come on in." James moved aside, knowing that Charles loathed being touched by another living thing.

"Now The Talk are back together."

"What in the name of God are you saying?" Miles drained his rum-and-coke, and showed that he needed another one.

Charles frowned. "I never liked that name. I still say we should have gone with the Blackbirds."

"Too faggy," Miles said. "And none of us are black."

"Well…." Charles scanned the living room. "What kind of party is this?"

"No party. What are you drinking, Charles?"

"Tea; green if you have it. Miles, are you still smoking?"

Miles lit up a Marlboro, looked around for an ashtray. "Am I breaking a rule?"

"No, smoke away," James said. "Here, use this bowl. It came from Greece."

"It doesn't look like an ashtray."

"Don't worry about it." James handed him the bronze urn decorated with gods and ancient grapes: "Melissa liked to buy things like this."

"Sorry about you and Melissa." Miles tapped his ash into the urn.

"Oh, well. How many times were you married, Miles?"

"Three."

"And you never did marry, Charles."

"Marriage is unsanitary."

They both studied James, expecting something. He had invited them over, after so many years…some kind of…important celebration?

"What do you think of the Come-Backs?"

After a stunned moment Charles and Miles both laughed in his face.

"Get me another drink. You can't be serious."

"Really stupid," Charles muttered. "There is no other band name stupider than that. Why not the Has Beens?"

"That's not as bad as you might think," Miles said. "A tongue-in-cheek kind of thing."

Charles stared at his wealthy host. "You lured us here to try and get the band together again? Tell me no, James."

"I'll ask you why not?" James got up to fix another drink for himself and Miles. When he returned he slapped a baggie and a pipe onto the antique walnut coffee table.

Charles stared. "Is that pot?"

"How long's it been since you were stoned?"

"Twenty years and nine months this January the First."

"Last night," Miles said. "What is this, James? Some mid-life desperation?"

"Call it that. When you were playing the drums, Miles—those scarred-up Slingerlands—and your arms were tentacles and your eyes were crazy. Remember? Being on stage and playing the music—remember?"

"I remember being alive. That was a while ago."

"So was I. My Stratocaster was alive in my hands. I was alive then, and I haven't been alive since."

"You're not thinking…" Charles stared at him. "No, I'm not going to smoke that. James, I'm sorry that you're going through a—crisis and all that. No, Miles! Take that marijuana away from me."

"Come on, Charles, aren't you tired of being afraid? Take a hit."

"Smoke pot with us, you pussy," Miles said.

There was always one of these quiet and stupid moments.

"You want to get the band together because of some dream you had." Charles recoiled at the idea. "I'm no pussy. I'm the greatest bass player who ever lived."

"I haven't hit a drum in ten years," Miles confessed.

"But don't you want to, one last time? Don't we want to be alive again one last time?"

Miles took a hard hit of the pipe, sucking the marijuana expertly in. "Charles, take a hit."

"No, I don't want to."

"You do! Take a hit or I'll kill you. I always wanted to kill you. You puss."

"I am not a puss." Charles took a hit, the sweet twenty year old past flowing into his lungs, the other world taking over.

"We're comfortable, that's the problem," Miles said. "We're all comfortable in our lives. You can't play music when you're comfortable."

"Are we?" James asked. "Or are we just scared? We're old and tired and scared. The stupid thing is, we no longer have anything to be scared of. All those years ago when we were climbing onto stages like crazy monkeys? We had everything to lose back then; we weren't afraid. Now we have nothing to lose—and we're afraid. But what do we have to lose?"

"I remember the girls," Charles said, his eyes going back. "Here, stop bogarting the weed, Miles. You bastard, you always bogarted the weed."

"I don't know about the name," Miles said, violently blowing smoke, cough and snot into the air. "The Come-Backs? CAWWWWW!!! It's gay."

"Well, what then?"

"Hey, we're The Talk," Charles said.

MILES COLEMAN...

WE ARE ALL MORTAL, wrote many an author. That hardly makes us special. Everything that *is* is mortal, even the long-suffering rocks. In measure, everything is equal: the coyote cannot sit in a room and stare at the wall, I cannot catch a rabbit. All things, living or not, are doomed to one day be no more. And yet, for all that, we still love. The force that makes the sea-bird mother's eyes stare so intensely back at her chick, who now dances to the end of the branch, flares out her beautiful young wings and finally leaps into the sky.

And how the sea-bird mother, heart in her throat, cries mournfully at the wind when the chick cannot fly and falls cracking onto the sea rocks, crushed and gone forever. All horror stories are death, the great horror of all. I would gladly have died before my child, my wife—so would you. The great horror of death is that it is not horror for me, but for those I loved. We clutch religion because we fear death. We believe in ghosts because we fear death. We grab anything because we fear it. The weak fear it for themselves, the strong for those they love. We all fear it, because it will come.

I could talk about how I felt when my wife and child were murdered, how I yelled at God and busted my fists against the walls of our living room, how I fell into black bloodiness, the ragged *I Live!* Madness…

But you want to hear a horror story. And I will tell you a true one: not a tale scribbled by a clever writer, sitting with his cigarettes and coffee, thinking, "How do I scare my readers? A monster? What monster?"

"Not this story. The monster is only the dream by which horror comes about. The horror is always death, the taking of everything."

Forgive me, I'm not myself tonight, I'm in pain. I've been roaring at God and the scabbed blood clogs my throat. Now I sit in the eleven o'clock night and drink whiskey—fast—in order to dull my mind. To destroy it if possible.

Forgive me. You want to read a horror story, not some grim memoir. So, a horror story it is:

Miles Coleman, he's your monster, but hardly the creature you would ever imagine. A good guy, really; very cool. No ugly ogre—far from a ghost. A clever realist. I like this guy, I'll buy him a drink, we'll talk.

We have to make our monsters ugly, eh? In order to write a good horror story? But I have found that by and large, ugly people are far better and less cruel and more beautiful than beautiful people. My wife Cheryl was over-weight and not beautiful.

On the side, at a company party, I overheard Miles Coleman call her fat and ugly—out of my ears, so he thought. I lost my soul at that moment because I nodded with the rest of them. But Cheryl was so good, and she made my life good, and we had a daughter, Molly...

It was too late; I had lost my soul.

If you want a true horror story, then look beyond the ugly and shocking things a writer will invent. True horror—true evil—is not ugly, it is beautiful. True horror is seductive. It's not a creature crunching across the pages, it slithers so beautiful and seductive.

Forgive me again. I'm trying to tell a horror story—and I will. But first—please—I need to tell you what horror is: that it has nothing to do with ugliness and everything to do with beauty.

All right, let me tell you a horror story:

"God does not exist," Miles Coleman said to me as we drank whiskey sours one night at the Pub. "I've never believed God was true."

"I agree completely," I said. "The belief in God is the fear of reality, nothing more."

"Sad to say, we are just organic creatures, all of us. We crave God. Maybe all living creatures do."

"A strange need, born out of fear of the unknown."

"No doubt," Miles Coleman said.

I enjoyed his company, a man who spoke of things that others feared. One who had the courage to shed superstition. But I did see that his eyes glittered at me like the eyes of a reptile. He was brilliant and handsome and magnetic, and I wondered why he would invite a guy like me out for a drink after work.

I felt flattered, I'll admit. And I admired one who so casually dismissed what others cringe in fear of, or only pretend to believe from a different fear. Yet his eyes were like reptile eyes. I tried to say that they were eyes that boldly saw the truth, as I did. Maybe they were too pale, too glittering. I found myself caught up in the discussion…

"Do you believe there are such things as good and evil?" he asked me.

"Not really. Good and evil are subjective terms, human inventions. A tiger claims for its meal a tiny new-born lamb. Is that evil? No, it's nature."

"Yes, nature." Miles Coleman peered at me. "There is no such thing as evil?"

"Well…scientifically, no; unless everything is evil."

"But what if evil can live in only one place, can only occupy one niche, one organism."

"I don't know what you mean."

"What if evil is real, and it lives—but in only one species?"

"Careful, you getting close to the Bible," I laughed. "Are you referring to evil as some virus or other that can only infect the human race?"

"Yes."

"I think that's unlikely."

Miles Coleman stared at me. Reptile eyes caught me in their glitter. "You wife called me a name at the last company party. She called me an evil bastard. Maybe she had too much to drink. Susan was her name?"

"No, Cheryl." I felt afraid suddenly. "I apologize for her."

"No need to. I'm pragmatic about things like that. She was right. I am a bastard, and, I am evil." Miles Coleman gave me a chilling, doll-eyed smile. "I'm the Lord of pragmatism."

I stared at him. "What do you mean?"

"You know the term pragmatism?"

"Yes. It's a cold and unbiased search for the truth."

"Is it." Miles Coleman stared away. "I got your—portly—wife's name wrong. But I'm sure the little girl was named Molly."

"What!"

"Do you think there is anything beyond pragmatism?" he asked.

I tried to think for a second: "No one's discovered it yet."

"You will discover it," Miles Coleman said.

"What do you mean? When?"

"When you get home tonight."

WITCH WANTED. APPLY INSIDE. . .

"M R. CRAWFORD, YOU ADVERTISED for a witch."
      I sat back at my desk, delighted to see her again. I thanked God, in fact. I'm no romantic by any stretch; I don't read novels, I watch football. But the first time I saw Miss Cromwell I fell madly in love with her.

She had returned only to get the disappointing news that she hadn't been selected to play the witch at Mr. Warren's Halloween Horror House. But, thank God Almighty, she had returned.

"I'm sorry, Miss Cromwell." I looked into her eyes; beautiful lavender blue.

She had a face of ancient beauty, unspoiled by cosmetics. Long, swirling hair, as black as oil, red lips and red cheeks. Her speech and mannerisms were so un-modern that I marveled at her acting skills.

"But I do not understand," she said. "The woman you hired is no witch."

"Well, I'm afraid Mr. Warren had the last say in the matter. I put a good word in for you, Miss Cromwell; but frankly, you're too beautiful to play a witch."

"But I am a witch. And the woman hired is not."

I smiled. "Mr. Warren wanted a—classical type witch. You know: ugly, hag-like, long warty nose, a good cackler. You're none of those things."

"Why then did you not advertise for a *false* witch, Mr. Crawford?"

"Look, you're too good an actress for this gig—much too pretty. I wondered yesterday why you'd ever want a job like this. Halloween witch for a month, in a local spook house?"

"You advertised for a witch," she said, with a bit of ice in her voice.

"I surely would have picked you for the part, Miss Cromwell. But old Warren wanted the stereotype."

"Pardon me?"

"A fun witch, not a scary one. Not that you're scary, by any means. But—well, you come across as too Victorian, you see. Too serious."

"Mr. Warren did not strike me as being a man who understands seriousness," she said.

"Look, this is a Halloween Horror House, but kids are going to show up there. They expect to see an ugly witch that cackles and rubs her bony hands, and—you know..."

"I do not cackle, Mr. Crawford."

I couldn't take my eyes off her. Stupid as it sounds, I was blind in love with her, and my heart wouldn't slow down. "Can I take you to lunch?" I blurted out. "Coffee? There's a good place..."

She gave me an arch look. "Why?"

"Well, because—okay, because I find you enchanting, and I'd like to get to know you. You're a very good actress, too good for a foolish gig like this. But I know some people: Agents, people looking for talent."

"Whatever made you believe that I am an actress, Mr. Crawford? I told you—I am a witch."

"You've certainly put a spell on me."

Dumb thing to say; and I knew I had a high school grin on my face.

"Lunch, dinner, a movie?" I stared desperately into her eyes.

She stood and favored me with a mysterious half-smile. "Not today. Another time, perhaps. Love spells are often dangerous. I should not toy with them so." She turned to leave my office and I felt despair that she would be gone.

From my life?

"Miss Cromwell—"

I jumped up, raking my thigh on the desk. I felt like an idiot; but I couldn't control the desire I felt for her. "I don't even know your first name."

"Elizabeth."

Her eyes had changed. They were penetrating now, near frightening. She was a brilliant actress.

"When can I see you again?"

"I am not sure. Spells are dangerous, and I shouldn't play with them. Curses are more dangerous, of course. Anyway, I thank you for putting in a good word with this Mr. Warren. He obviously does not believe in witches, or curses. He should not have advertised for a witch if he did not want one."

"Miss Cromwell—please!"

But she was gone.

I stared out the window of my office until she appeared on the street below. I watched her vanish into the faceless crowds flowing about the city.

My God, I thought. How beautiful—what an actress!

The door squawked open, jarring me out of my dream, and Benny came into the office. He wore a strange face.

I turned to him. "I finally met the love of my life, Old Boy!" I roared at him. "They say it's a stupid myth, falling in love at first sight. But at first sight I met the woman I want to spend the rest of my life with. She's very—well, unusual. A very good actress." I looked at him. "What's wrong?"

"You haven't heard?" Benny asked. "Mr. Warren had a heart attack this morning. He didn't make it. Mr. Warren's dead!'"

THREE KINDS OF MONSTER...

SOMETIMES YOU HAVE EVERYTHING and the bastard still walks.

That was my big worry with the Amy Torres murder: that Dane Lowenstein would walk away again with that sad, innocent look on his movie-star mask, as if he couldn't understand how anyone would ever accuse him of such a crime.

I practically lived at Homicide, making myself a trembling, coffee-stealing pain in the ass; and despite Anthony Payne's frequent pats on the back and therapeutic assurances that "We got him, Jack", I didn't trust the system to work.

Dane Lowenstein had murdered before, in exactly the same way, and he had walked.

Anthony Payne was a good detective; he was a black man, tall and imposing and forged in the world of assumptions, where women clutch their purses when they pass him and unfamiliar cops study him in his crisp suit and tie. Anthony had been around long enough to see through the blond Nordic charm of a creature like Dane Lowenstein. But a jury had not been able to before—could they now?

Most of the detectives hated but tolerated me. A private investigator (they called us *Creepers*), was a mere step away from criminal in their code. They hated my hanging around and my sarcastic interference and my doubting of their abilities. I was the *creeper* who had put them on the trail of Dane Lowenstein, and so they naturally thought I was trying to steal their thunder on this case; and as I said before, I really was making myself a pain in the ass. I tried to make them see that I only wanted justice, but most of them had been around long enough to roll their eyes at the word.

"Justice is revenge with a married name," Anthony said to me; his wood-colored eyes reminded me of alcohol and cigarettes and sleepless nights. "You've been obsessed with this toad too many years, Brother. Now pat yourself on the back and relax. Go home, watch porn or something. You'll get your revenge, Jack, I promise. We got this boy. Don't worry; he's going away for good."

"I don't care if it's justice or revenge. I don't care about credit. I don't even care what your *colleagues* think of me. All I want is for this bastard to pay. Tell me he's going to pay—Brother."

"My colleagues are pissed because you nailed the guy and they didn't." Anthony laughed, but there wasn't much humor there. "I can't tell you what we got, Jack. But believe me, it's enough. He's in the cage downtown, he ain't going anywhere."

Anthony didn't have to tell me what they'd found, I already knew: fingerprints from a glass in Amy's apartment, a hair fiber on her couch that matched Lowenstein's DNA.

But it only proved that he was there in her place. That alone didn't prove he was the killer. I had seen a jury turn away from hard evidence before and sigh at Lowenstein's angelic face and decide that *He couldn't have done such a thing.*.

"You need to let it go now," Anthony said to me. "Let the system work, Jack."

"What, are you all at once a champion of the system? Do I have to tell you about the system?"

Anthony sighed and stared out the windows at the city, an orderly grey and green promise of civilization: "We got this pretty-boy. You were right all along. He can smile and charm any jury in the world, but he ain't walking this time; too much evidence, I don't care how many women are sitting in those chairs."

"With Dane Lowenstein, there's never too much evidence," I reminded him.

"Go home, Jack. Celebrate in your own—way." Anthony rubbed my shoulder with his gentle paw. "Leave it be for awhile."

I walked into the bright day, stepping down the granite steps of the City-County building, where prosecuting attorneys and defense attorneys marched past like carefully-dressed machines—home to what?

I stopped at Walmart on the way to get a quart of whiskey, the cheapest, Canadian Club. I wondered what club I was joining. I suppose it wasn't a true quart, because the Canadians used the metric system, didn't they? But it would work.

I unlocked the cheap brass bolt to my apartment and shoved open the plywood door. The sun was still blazing across a mild spring sky, and I twisted shut the plastic curtains, gaining some darkness, some promise of oblivion.

I mixed the cheap whiskey with cheaper Coke and settled down in my daily ritual to the gods of oblivion. Pot would help, it would make me feel better; but I was out, and it seemed too much of a chore to call Stacey and get more. I had plenty of cigarettes and enough booze; that should be enough for today.

I stared at the plastic curtains that covered the windows of my smelly apartment. The sun wanted in, maybe to penetrate darkness—God wanting to get in. I sipped the terrible whiskey and coke and waited for oblivion. God could wait until He finally gave me justice.

After all, it was God who had created the 10 year old boy who skillfully shot the eyes out of birds with his bee-bee gun; who tied kittens onto his mother's clothesline so that he could douse them with gasoline from the five gallon plastic jug his dad kept in the garage for the lawnmower; who at age 15 had been caught by a neighbor feeding baby rabbits into his dad's wood-chipper, laughing his joy at the squeals and frantic cries of the little things, nodding his handsome, ash-blond head at the crunched bones, the bloody-hairy red spittle that vomited out of the roaring machine.

Hey, God: thanks so very much for Dane Lowenstein.

Anthony Payne, a seasoned detective, had suspicion in his eyes whenever he talked to me about this case, why it was driving me so crazy to see Dane Lowenstein caged

forever. But I couldn't tell Anthony the truth. I'm not obsessed with justice; I'm a simple loser who makes his living spying on people, putting the final period to divorce papers, showing folks the ugly truth for money—that's all I am.

Don't get me wrong; I'm good at what I do. I abuse pot and alcohol when I can (which is always), I smoke way too many cigarettes and maybe hope some day my vices will kill me. But I'm good at what I do. And now I'm at the pathetic point where I only want my life to mean something. I only want to remove from the world a monster, so that he can never again destroy another innocent human life. I tell myself this as I sip at the whiskey and stare at the glowing plastic window. I can die with a smile if I know I've saved some innocent in the future from the horror of that monster. So there, God.

(A lie, maybe).

Amy Torres wasn't innocent, not in the Christian sense. She had her problems, her demons. She had drug problems, that's how I met her. And she had performed sex for money. I knew this when I spied on her years ago, and gave her husband cause for divorce. This was before I fell in love with her.

Well, that was years ago, and my delusions about the monster Dane Lowenstein wanting revenge against me were just that, paranoid delusions. It was a coincidence that he targeted her because…or was it?

I had tried to nail him for a similar murder two years ago, the bloody stabbing of a young college girl; and he had walked, giving me a brilliant and knowing wink outside the courthouse as he passed into the sunlight. How could he have ever found out that I was in love with Amy Torres? No, I was giving this creature too much credit.

Or was I? Things like him never forget. Things like him find an arch-enemy and discover secrets somehow. They delve into their foes, making a study, finding secrets. Things like him do not forget enemies, and I knew Dane Lowenstein was smart—brilliant even. Could he have known that I once loved Amy? I couldn't underestimate something like him, an evil energy. Every morning I would stare at my ragged face in the mirror and remind myself that he was smarter than I was.

They say that only once in your life do your eyes see the one you will truly love forever. It was like that with Amy. And I ruined her life, leaving her in wretched misery while her relieved husband wrote me the check.

I loved her and she hated me, and I went on knowing I would never get her face out of my mind. It was like the tragic scene where you see your destiny in the face of another, where you see redemption and hope and promise, even some magic; when God gives you the one chance to take the right path; and then you walk away from her down the wrong path because you destroyed her and she hates you; and then you simply get drunk. And then your drunken mind knows suddenly that you have missed happiness, you have missed everything, and it will never return. That was what it was like with Amy Torres.

Now she was as dead as we all will be, dead under the ground, skeletonizing like the eyeless birds the monster had once brought to ground with his air rifle. I could only have revenge now, I could never have redemption. If Dane Lowenstein tortured and murdered her to get revenge against me—or not—if it was a cruel coincidence or not, my only reason to exist came down to revenge. If I met Dane Lowenstein in Hell I would at least have that. I would never have Amy. Jack Smith goes on with his work because he's a born <u>Creeper</u>, nothing more.

Now that I'm fairly drunk, let me tell you about Dane Lowenstein and what I know of creatures like him: In the old days it was simply said that some people were good and some were evil. But our modern world began to take a closer look at subjects like Dane Lowenstein, and they questioned such knee-jerk assumptions about good and evil. Psychiatry in the 20th Century made many studies of these strange individuals—walking, breathing demons—and they came up with a name: <u>Psychopath</u>.

The term felt right, because it explained away so many fears: it was not evil or the devil at work inside these individuals; it was a traumatic childhood that had made them so deviant, so sadistic.

A tormented childhood was what created evil people. This explanation felt good, because it gave the promise that things could be reversed, that proper treatment could cure these unfortunate folks and mold them into good human beings.

Babies are all born innocent, psychiatry assured the fearful public. Childhood trauma was to blame. This was not far from the religious view, except religion blamed Satan and not trauma. No one ever believed that a child could simply have been born evil, religion and psychiatry be damned.

Who can say what is true?

Psychiatry eventually decided that it was counter-productive to label these unfortunate individuals psychopaths, the term was too scary, too judgmental, too—Alfred Hitchcock. A better term was sociopath, more buttered-up and acceptable: a class of suffering people who had no concept of right and wrong, of conscience. If they made others suffer, it was only because they themselves were suffering—childhood trauma, low self-esteem, that sort of thing. Evil never butted into their theories, and that was a good turn for evil. It is always content to sit and wait when academic folly gives it what it wants. Yes! We only need to be treated, to be understood—then we'll be good.

Following his arrest for the murder of Carla Houseman two years ago (a student at the university), I was determined to interview Dane Lowenstein: At the time I was considering—shamelessly—researching a book on sociopaths; and while he was in custody I depended on Anthony to let that happen. Dane had to agree, of course. I knew he would—I knew sociopaths that well; their need to encounter "experts" who really didn't know shit. Anyway, two years ago I sat with the beast in a bolted-down yellow-and-green steel cage at the state mental hospital and gazed into his shark-blue eyes. I had to prepare myself for the possibility that this guy might actually walk away free from the horror he had done, he was that convincing. And I saw in his eyes that he recognized me as his greatest enemy. He was delighted that I wasn't a true badge; only a private investigator with a license you could get from a magazine.

Such a dimpled, charming smile he gave to me—any girl would quickly melt. He could have been a model, a movie star:

"Glad to meet you, Jack," he said, not bothering to extend a hand. "So you're the knight on the horse."

"I'm the knight on the horse, Dane."

He studied me, and I felt weak, feeling a cold power beyond mine.

"You get paid for window-peeking, Jack. Who paid you to look into me?"

"Nobody. It's pro bono for the world, to get you locked away."

"I won't be locked away," Dane said calmly. "I'm innocent."

"You're innocent. Let's see....you know, I've heard that before."

He let out a charming laugh: "That's right." His handsome face studied me. A bright Nazi power bloomed in his eyes, a god certainty. I was a bug he was having fun with. "I've never killed anybody, Jack. My apologies, but that's the truth. I don't kill people. I'm not a murderer."

"I can read lies," I warned him.

Dane Lowenstein nodded and studied me, his blue eyes blinking with thought. "You're not a badge—sorry. You always wanted to be, but you had to settle for Pretend Cop."

"That's right; I'm one of those irritating little private investigators who dig where the cops don't. I'm not ashamed of that."

"Did you get your license from one of those cereal boxes?"

"I got my license from your mother's ass," I told him. "Don't try to con a con, Dane. That'll be good advice where you're going."

"I'm going home, Jack," he said, smiling at me. "And then what?"

I took a long breath. How much did he know about me? How could he know anything about me?

"I *am* a con," he said at last. "I'm a good con, so? I do my research. But I'm not a murderer. I can't stand the smell of blood. You're the P.I. who dug up all this evidence against me."

"Yes, Dane, I am."

"Ah. Well, you dug up the wrong guy, Jack, because I never killed Amy Torres or anybody else."

"Is that why you're under psychiatric evaluation, to see if you're sane enough to stand trial?"

"I'm sane enough to stand trial—and I'll be found <u>not</u> guilty."

"How so?"

His blue eyes fondled mine. He brushed a strand of Hitler hair from his face. "Two reasons, Jack," he said. "One; I'm a con, a better one than you. And I know from experience that the easiest person in the world to con is a psychiatrist. I've been evaluated by a lot of psychiatrists, and they're all educated to the point of being morons. It's no big trick to con a psychiatrist; they're all desperate to prove they're real doctors. And two: I'll walk because I'm innocent. I've committed crimes, and so have you, Jack. But I've never murdered anybody."

And he did walk.

I poured another 80/20 whiskey and coke into my plastic glass, trying to carve the past out of my memory. I've come up with the theory that there are three kinds of human monsters. The first is the most harmless: he's the one who has no conscience but also fears violence. This sneaky and cowardly human will take from the innocent what he needs and feel no remorse; a scared worm who makes sadness for a living but goes no further, because violence and death are too far. These creatures can't make you believe much.

The Second ones are those who take and feel no remorse; who create pain and suffering not because they want to, but because it is necessary at a certain moment. They will kill you if you get in the way of their evil, their bank robbery or whatever, but they will not kill you if you stand aside. If you let them do evil they will spare your life—if you try and stop them they will kill you. These creatures don't care if you believe in them or not.

Dane Lowenstein was the third kind of evil: That is evil that <u>wants</u> evil; that demands it. These are creatures that kill not because it is necessary but because it is fun. Evil is not the price of doing business, it is the reward. For these things evil is crack cocaine, and <u>everything</u> that exists does so in order to give to them the greatest thrill of all, the pain and suffering of living things. These are the ones who can make you trust anything.

I don't believe in vampires, or even monsters. I use the name not in any supernatural sense. I don't believe anything supernatural exists. However, I've been in this business long enough to know that evil suffocates our planet. I wish it were not so, but it is. And my drunken, loser existence only hangs onto the hope that I can somehow fight against evil. Call it revenge, call it a last gift to Amy Torres, the love of my wretched life—I don't care what you call it.

I stared at the floor. A great sociopath like Dane Lowenstein, with so many physical powers and sexual powers…you women who are reading this would believe what he told you, he would make you believe. Call me a sexist, but you would believe. His power is to *make* you believe.

Let's call them <u>sociopaths</u> if that watered-down term pleases you. I can tell you this; and it all has to do with our sick television society: the ugly ones, brilliant or not, are sitting on prison bunks; the beautiful ones, but stupid, wind up girl-boys on the same prison bunks.

However, the beautiful and brilliant ones can go on and on torturing and destroying, and society will forgive them, because we never see beyond their beauty, their charm. It is as if our television brains <u>want</u> them to go free.

These are the true monsters. They can lie to you all day, and all day you will believe them.

A monster tortured and destroyed the only woman I have ever loved. I know who the monster is, and I used every skill I have to bring him to you, the good public, although none of you will ever know it. You the jury will see Dane Lowenstein, and you'll be captivated by his beauty and bewildered, dimpled face. You'll never in your life believe that this blond cherub could have torn apart another human being, a young girl who wanted love, in who's eyes I finally saw love.

But listen to this: These creatures have the ability to beguile you, to force you to see that what is not true <u>is</u> true. I'm now getting drunk and falling into oblivion. Goodbye for now. But listen: There are real creatures stepping over this earth that can make you believe that evil is good. I've met so many of them that my stomach burns and wants to puke up. Call them psychopaths or sociopaths or whatever you want. But don't be fooled.

I prayed that the jury would be wise enough to see this. Then I fell into oblivion.

Thank you, God. Beyond all hopes and prayers, Dane Lowenstein and his attorney made the biggest mistake of their lives at his trial:

My biggest fear—and Ant's, I knew—was that Lowenstein would admit that he knew Amy Torres, that he had been to her apartment, yes, but that was all. He knew her, he had touched a glass there and left a hair sample—but he had not killed her, he could never do a thing like that.

The jury might have believed his solemn, beautiful face when he demanded to testify on his own behalf.

Instead, he performed the stupidest act he could have—and it left me stunned. He denied ever knowing Amy Torres. He denied ever being in her apartment. He accused the police of planting the finger-printed glass and hair sample. He denied having ever <u>met</u> the victim.

His lawyer made a lame attempt to convince the jury that the water glass with his client's fingerprints all over it was not consistent with the other drinking glasses in Amy's apartment (as if that carried any weight). And regarding the hair fiber—well, DNA was a questionable science at best…

After so many nights of misery and worry, I finally glimpsed hope. I smelled the impossible blood of victory. When the word uttered from the jury foreman "Guilty" splashed over me like a warm ocean wave, I slumped in my chair, shuddering with relief—I welcomed God again.

Dane Lowenstein stood now, finally, like one of the frightened baby rabbits in front of the judge, in front of God and humanity, all of his power suddenly gone. The demon would be caged, and another monster would be deprived of its feeding ground. I dared not believe that I had won.

I had not saved Amy, so the verdict was bitter at best; I would take flowers to her lonely grave and say how much I loved her, and I was sorry, sorry, sorry…that was all I could do now.

"It's over!" I slapped hands with Anthony when he came up to me. We watched Dane Lowenstein shuffle away, handcuffed, into oblivion. "I love you, Brother. We finally saw justice this day."

Anthony looked at me, his eyes sad. "You got your thing, Brother," he replied.

"We need to celebrate, Ant. Let's go have a drink."

"Naw. I'm not in the mood for celebrating."

I saw that something in his eyes. But it didn't worry me. The great monster of my life, Dane Lowenstein, was gone, shuffling away in steel chains, his blue Nordic eyes stunned with disbelief. I would drink tonight to his downfall, to Amy's beautiful face, to the justice that I never believed I would ever see. I would drink to God tonight, and thank Him for what I never thought I'd see—justice.

A sociopath has unique abilities to make you believe that a lie is the truth. Anyone can fall prey, even the smartest juror. No one is immune to these creatures—I know that from bitter experience. Thank God these were jurors who actually read the evidence.

But enough of that for now: The world was suddenly wonderful again. Ant had his suspicions, as I knew he would. But I had planted seeds and covered bases that I knew would stay covered. I remembered the sound of those little rabbits.

SECOND CHANCE...

"**N**EBRASKA'S ONE OF THE last states to still use the electric chair. Did you know that?"

"Yes. A barbaric practice." The pastor looked away. He couldn't say there was fear in John Elritch's face, only a pale sort of shock. "God willing we will be able to abolish it forever."

"The electric chair."

"Capital punishment altogether. God willing."

"God willing."

"Have you…" The pastor fingered the Bible on his lap. "Are you prepared, John?"

"I'm not sure. You were going to ask me if I've repented? Yes. Not one second has passed since that day that I haven't—at least regretted. I suppose repentance and regret are close to the same thing."

"We're hoping for a reprieve."

John nodded but said nothing. He was functioning, yet numb. He seemed to see the world, the cement cell and yellow bars, out of the wrong end of a telescope. Years of waiting in a cage, now…He buzzed with a strange white noise all the way through his senses—like hearing and seeing things after an explosion has damaged membranes.

"Do you want to talk about that day?"

The condemned stared away. He searched for something. The pastor had seen eyes like this at the hospice. But this was different. These eyes seemed to be seeking not beyond, but before.

John looked down at the Bible in the pastor's lap. "You believe in second chances."

"Redemption."

"Not redemption, true second chances."

"What do you mean?"

John stared at the electric light above the *Death Cell.* "That if God is all-powerful, He can grant a true second chance. That He can take you back through time and start the clock again and give you a chance to take another path."

"I believe God can do anything. But He gives us the power to choose, and we must live with our choices. And we must—"

"Pay for them." John nodded at the light. "It's not a matter of trying to avoid punishment. And I understand what you mean by second chances. Say if that phone would ring and the governor would spare my life—give me a second chance—that I could then spend the rest of my life in a cell trying to do good and atone for that day twenty years ago. That's what you mean by God giving second chances."

"Yes."

"I don't mean that. I mean if God would actually take you back. If God would…never mind. You asked me if I wanted to talk about that day. I was twenty years old. I'd buddied up with a guy I never should have, Billy Jones. I knew he was a psycho, but I admired his balls, how he didn't take anything off anybody. I admired how scared people were of him. He got respect, and when I hung out with him I got respect too. I had a girlfriend, her name was Allison. My mom always asked me why I'd hang out with a criminal like Billy instead of Allison. I suppose it was that rush of adrenaline or something, playing the bad boy when I wasn't.

"I never knew how bad Billy was until that day. He drove a hot Mustang fastback, and riding around in it, I felt ballsy and powerful. That day Billy wanted to drink, but we didn't have money for booze. He pulled the Mustang into a 7-11 and got a pistol out of the glove box. I knew he was going to commit a robbery, and I could have bolted. But once I got into that car, it was all over. I didn't want to be a wuss, I didn't want Billy Jones coming after me. So I sat there and waited.

"When I heard the three gunshots, I knew something had happened. Billy ran out of the store and we roared away."

"Three people murdered," the pastor said.

"Only one older than me."

"That's your hope for reprieve, John: You didn't kill anyone."

"These last twenty years I've thought that if I hadn't got into that car, if I'd gone over to Allison's instead..."

The pastor stared away. He had never tried to counsel a man who was only minutes away from execution.

But now it was time. John was escorted down the death hall and into a room where sat a medieval wooden chair. Brown leather straps hung from the chair's legs and armrests, and a silver bowl sprouting wires was suspended above. Beyond a glass screen observers peered. John saw the pastor there, the man worriedly glancing at the telephone on the wall.

Electric chair. A terrifying name

Guards strapped him down and lowered the bowl onto his head. Everything appeared distant, telescopic. He waited for the jolt.

The phone rang.

No, it wasn't the phone. He jumped awake, stared at the light above his bedroom. A car horn.

He bolted out of bed and stared out the window of his bedroom.

"John," his mother called from up the stairs. "Is that Billy out there?"

He rubbed his eyes, let out a deep breath. "Yeah, Mom. We're going out for awhile."

"Allison called."

"Tell her I'll call her back."

He got dressed and went out to the cool Nebraska morning. He got into the Mustang and took the cigarette Billy offered him. The car screeched away. He thought of Allison, and he shuddered.

Billy looked over at him. "What's with you? You look wussed-out."

"I had a weird dream, that's all."

IVY BOULEVARD. . ..

"I HAVE TO ADMIT," Dr. Keller said. "Not without some twinge of conscience—that a noted psychiatrist who finds himself a patient in the State Mental Hospital is an interesting study. I hope you'll forgive me for being so blunt, Dr. Ridley; but your case is baffling."

The noted Dr. Ridley had a twisted smile on his face that made the stomach curl. "You're supposed to refer to it as a Regional Center, Dr. Keller, not mental hospital. How telling that our particular profession changes its terms so often in order to cater to the squeamish public. But I do forgive you. Mad becomes feeble-minded becomes mentally-challenged becomes patient becomes client. Evil becomes psychopath becomes sociopath becomes childhood trauma—as if by changing the terms we could ever change anything. I forgive you. If our places were reversed, I assure you that I'd study you also with morbid fascination."

Dr. Keller studied him with—yes, morbid fascination. Who couldn't? And above them were the animal sounds of the top ward, bellows and calls and tiresome psychotic rants and wails; stomping feet, echoes off the steel doors and concrete walls. The ward called S-5, where the violently mad and criminally insane wriggled together in a hell-box of yellow containment. Yes, morbid fascination, for here in his office was a distinguished psychiatrist, former elbow-rubber with the governor and other men of power, who looked so mortally weak in bile-green pajamas, his feet in spongy state slippers. This was a man—a colleague, thought Keller, with some undeserved hubris—who had not long ago commanded a salary of over 500,000 dollars a year. An eminent psychiatrist who now so resembled the other shuffling wretches from S-5, ugly creatures either pretending to be insane, or truly lost in the vortex of madness.

Are we so much the appearance of our clothes? He thought.

Dr. Ridley seemed unconcerned about his wraithlike and slightly stinky presentation. He peered at Dr. Keller out of telescopic eyeglasses that widened his brown eyes. He kept that spooky smile on his face, and he did seem mad.

Keller let the silence gather. Finally it was Dr. Ridley who spoke: "You're wondering, of course, if I've diagnosed my own condition."

"Yes, I am."

"I have. But first we should talk a little about judgments."

"Judgments."

"Isn't that what so much of our profession relies upon? For instance, I was a private psychiatrist with a smooth and glittery office downtown. I was respected, admired, safe in a small mansion on Ivy Boulevard. You are a state psychiatrist. Would it not be logical to assume that I might feel superior to you—that my mind might be tempted to think you took a job in this hell because you couldn't succeed in the private sector?"

Dr. Keller stared at him, appalled. "We're not here to discuss my career," he said.

"But these judgments are quite important, Dr. Keller. You, on the other hand, are liable to judge me an elitist, a Beverly Hills sort of psychiatrist who specialized in milking a good living from safe, neurotic rich people; a doctor who took the easy and lucrative way, never having to analyze or treat the monsters, the truly, hideously insane—or worse, the criminal pretenders?"

"All that is interesting, Dr. Ridley; but beside the point. You can only satisfy the state by explaining how you could do what you did."

"How? With a common butcher knife; you know this."

"Let me rephrase: *why* did you commit this crime?"

"Your job, Doctor, is to analyze my mental condition at the moment of the crime. So you should be the one to answer that question: whether I'm sane enough to stand trial, or whether I require more treatment in order to be sane enough to stand trial in the future and then be sentenced to death. Maybe together we can arrive at the diagnosis."

Keller stared into the owl eyes peering so strangely out of the expensive, designer glasses. He studied the smile that Ridley kept fixed on his face.

"I can only form an analysis of your mental condition if you speak openly to me. This crime, Dr. Ridley…well, a state psychiatrist or not, my duty is…why am I explaining to you? You know what I have to determine."

"Of course. If I was legally insane at the time of the felony."

"Felony….yes."

The smile disturbed him more than any expression of madness Keller had ever encountered. He had studied many horrors in his career. He had trained himself to determine if the horrors were truly insane or pretending in order to avoid prison. But this was different, and he seemed to stare into something beyond common horror.

Before him in his office was Dr. Milton Ridley, a wealthy and respected psychiatrist, author of two celebrated books, one on the career of Sigmund Freud, the other a case study of serial murderers, a man earning more than a half million dollars a year. Dr. Ridley had one dark and half-moon night wandered from his mansion on Ivy Boulevard down the manicured sidewalk and approached the home of the Fergusen family, a wealthy Ivy Boulevard couple with two young children. Dr. Ridley knocked on the door of the house and when Mrs. Fergusen answered he immediately stabbed her to death. He then entered the house, where Mr. Fergusen lay snoring on the couch. Ridley slashed the man's throat all the way to the spinal column, sending sprays of blood in every direction. Ridley used a very expensive serrated graphite knife borrowed from his wife's kitchen. She fancied herself a chef.

Now Mr. and Mrs. Fergusen lay dead and bloody in their clean suburban mansion. But a sound came from up the stairs. A two year old boy and a six year old girl lay sleeping up there. Dr. Milton Ridley's footsteps made no sound as they climbed the carpeted stairs.

In the boy's room, Spongebob Squarepants grinned from a poster; the walls were painted sky-blue with white clouds. He butchered the little Fergusen boy, then quietly padded into the daughter's room, where Hannah Montana smiled at him from the girl-pink wall. There was no sign of rape or any physical abuse other than the pure butchery that left the six-year-old girl a pile of death.

Dr. Keller had learned to harden his mind by using the technique called *compartmentalizing*. How else to coldly and accurately make a diagnosis that would satisfy a Mental Health Board or a jury? Humans often commit acts of horror that emotion cannot yield to analysis—he didn't have that luxury. He had forgone that luxury long ago—but what kind of madness was this?

"You should begin by telling me what happened to you, Dr. Ridley," he said at last. "If you're to present any kind of case for Temporary Insanity, you must tell me what happened to you."

"What happened to me…on that night…" Dr. Ridley aimed his crazed smile at the yellow-painted concrete wall. "I can't blame you; if our roles were reversed—"

"No, don't say that. Our roles are not reversed. You're not helping your cause by smiling at me like a ghoul, Dr. Ridley. Either try to explain to me what happened to you that night, or not. You destroyed, in a most brutal way, a family; a mother, a father and two young children. Do you not see that?"

"Yes, of course I see it. Do I understand it? You're the state's expert psychiatrist, Dr. Keller. So you must tell me why I did it."

Keller paused, staring at the smile. "Temporary Insanity, brought on by some extreme stress," he said.

"Ah, very good. Very expected. What about evil?"

"Evil. You never exhibited any signs of evil before the crime. At any rate, you know as well as I do that evil isn't a diagnosis that would stand up in court."

"True. Another term we've managed to water away down the drain."

"Let's get beyond our *terms* and come down to business. You snapped, obviously. In some way your brain, your psyche, your sense of right and wrong snapped. Can you tell me why?"

"Why a distinguished psychiatrist would destroy his life and his career? Why he would destroy an innocent family, why he would butcher children?"

"Yes. You've spent your life analyzing mental illnesses. Surely you have some—insights."

"Answers, you mean?" Dr. Ridley stared at the yellow concrete walls. "No one has answers to these things, Dr. Keller. But I do have a theory."

"I would advise, if you're hoping for a diagnosis of Temporary Insanity, that you tell me this theory."

Dr. Ridley thought for a moment. "Hmm, Temporary Insanity. First used by Edwin Stanton, later Secretary of War in the Abraham Lincoln administration, in the trial of Daniel Sickles, later to become a celebrated Civil War general, who had murdered the son of Francis Scott Keyes, author of The Star Spangled Banner, after the son had an affair with Sickle's wife. The son, by the way, Philip Keyes, was himself a U.S. District Attorney. That alone sounds like a delusional statement, doesn't it?"

(Was this man trying to test him?)

"No," said Keller. "I've read of the case."

"Then you know it was successful."

"Yes."

"I see by your expression, Doctor, that you think I'm trying to impress you with a display of intellect."

"Are you?"

Dr. Ridley shrugged. "I'm trying to give you what you want. Criminals, if they hope to avoid prison, always try to give the therapist what they want."

(A slight, in the term "Therapist"?)

"You spoke earlier of judgments, Dr. Ridley. Is this some kind of judgment?"

"Of course." Ridley stared around him at the yellow state walls, ninety percent prison and only ten percent hospital: "I interned in this very building many years ago; and I know that the general rule is that the doctor interview patients on the ward, in the *Conference Room*—another modern misnomer—as I've seen you do many times. Yet here I am in your very office."

(A touch of contempt—amusement?)

Dr. Keller frowned. He had only now met this eminent psychiatrist, but he had read both of Dr. Ridley's books. He had expected a brilliant but deeply troubled and depressed individual, maybe with a little leftover arrogance—but not this.

"It's a Spartan office," he said. "Hardly glittery, and not smooth."

"You see, that's where judgment comes in," said Ridley. "I'm being allowed to endure my psychiatric evaluation in your private office and not on the ward because you judge me special, because of who I am—or was. A judgment, you see."

"True, in part," Keller conceded. "I wanted quiet, and S-5 is never quiet."

"Very true. Also, I suspect, you're considering, or even endeavoring to write a book; and I'll probably make a very interesting chapter."

Dr. Keller frowned again. "My duty is to determine your mental state at the time you committed these homicides. Having said that, I also hope you can give me your professional insights concerning motivation, or lack of. You don't strike me as having any sense of remorse over what you've done."

"Ah, that makes me a garden-variety sociopath."

"I haven't decided; your disturbing smile indicates a mind not altogether in touch with reality."

"Oh, does it. Reality….hmm. Forgive me, I'll have to remember to frown now and again."

"You do display the arrogance of a sociopath, but investigations into your past and interviews with your family members and former colleagues give no signs of sociopathy up to the actual commission of the murders. Nothing in your past seems to indicate that you would be capable or desirous of committing such terrible acts. Yet here you sit chatting with me as if were having a talk over coffee. No history of mental illness, drug abuse—"

"No alcohol, tobacco or drug use. Well, I've got Freud beat there."

"So, let's get to the point, Dr. Ridley: You know the obvious first question."

"Why ever did I do it?"

"It seems at the least monstrously out of character."

Ridley shrugged. "Another judgment call. What is character? What is normal behavior? Only what we judge it to be."

"Doctor, the intellectual gamesmanship is all very interesting; but we're speaking of the vicious murders of 4 people: an innocent husband, a wife, two innocent children: or did you in some way *judge* them guilty of something?"

"No, I didn't judge them. I didn't even know them."

"Can you tell me what was going through your mind at the time you committed these murders?"

Ridley studied him for some moments, the eyes unmoving behind the thick glasses. Finally he said, "What if I told you that nothing was in my mind?"

"Is that the truth?"

"Yes. Nothing that I recall."

"You suffered some sort of black-out."

"Apparently. I woke up to a scream. I was in my own bed in my house at 536 Ivy Boulevard. The scream was my wife reacting to the blood that was smeared over the bed."

Dr. Keller had been writing in Ridley's chart. Now he paused and stared off. "Had you ever had black-out periods before?"

"No."

"Then surely, when you came to realize what you had done, you wanted to find answers."

"I had dreams afterwards. I dreamed I was a cougar killing a small deer. A deer is most vulnerable in its little familiar glen, grazing on thick spring grass. When you go into the world you have a heightened sense of danger—subconsciously, perhaps—if only the caution of driving a car. But when you're at home you have very little sense of danger—"

"Forgive me for interrupting you, Dr. Ridley," said Keller, wanting to regain control of what he felt was going to become a ramble. "If your mind was a total blank, how could you have had the presence to knock on the Fergusen's door?"

"As our good friend Freud suggested, the human mind can operate without conscious awareness. It seems there is another form of consciousness at work in some cases."

"So you dreamed that you were a cougar; and did you dream that the Fergusen family were the deer?"

"Yes. I can only speculate that that is why I used a knife."

"To simulate teeth."

"Yes. It's a very primitive way to kill—very organic. I had dreams afterwards of how the blade tore into the human flesh and organs. Also, a knife is very easy to conceal. Maybe more like a retractable claw than a tooth. The point is—and this is only a theory—that the mind can trip and fall into a state of awareness that returns it to a primitive state."

"The id."

Dr. Ridley frowned at last: "I never liked that term; far too simplistic. Let's leave it a primitive state. The animal from ages ago that hides—or is suppressed—inside all our minds. In rare cases it is somehow unleashed and manages to overcome our consciousness and seize control. R.L. Stevenson wrote about the condition, inventing Dr. Jekyll and Mr. Hyde; and I believe he was more intuitive than Freud, whom I've always considered over-rated. My conscious mind felt confusion after it returned, even a distant horror. But it could not summon guilt, because my conscious mind knows that it did not commit these crimes. Another pilot was driving the body.

"Now, the body should be punished for such an act, of course. But the primitive state that drove the body has gone back into its lair—and wouldn't, at any rate, even know that it was being punished."

Keller looked up from his writing. "You'll forgive me, Dr. Ridley, if that sounds to me like 'The devil made me do it'."

Ridley nodded. "I admit it's merely a theory. One, I suppose, to explain the unexplainable."

"So your returned conscious and sane mind didn't realize what you'd done?"

"It hasn't got the ability. Oh, I could pretend remorse, as so many do. But the truth is, my conscious mind refuses to believe that I murdered those people, those children. It's as if I'd read about it in the papers; as if I were accused of committing a crime I hadn't committed—even though I know very well that I did. A very nightmarish condition."

"Yes, it must be."

"But I can tell you a worse one: it has to do with my research on serial killers. When once this primitive state envelopes you and has its awful first romp in the sun, and then goes back into its dark corner, it recedes less further; as if it's come awake, and more restraint is needed to keep it back; as if it's only resting now, gathering its strength so that again some day it can..."

"Do you feel that happening, Dr. Ridley?"

"I sense it."

"So that once again in the future your conscious mind will black-out and this other mind will take control and force your body to kill again. That it wants to kill again?"

"It *needs* to."

Keller nodded. "A fascinating theory, I'll admit. Not original, you know. The theory has been proposed by many experts; proposed by serial killers themselves."

"Well, they should know the phenomenon. Only a theory, though. It remains that I'm guilty of an unspeakable crime."

"But you don't fully accept that you committed it."

"Well, if what I *am* is my body, then yes, I certainly committed it. But if what I *am* is my conscious mind, then I did not."

Keller paused for a few moments. "Let's go back to this dream: the cougar, the deer."

"Yes. Well, going on with the theory: In its most primitive state, the mind only wants to satisfy the body. We experience this every day, but our modern and civilized brains manage to trick it away—like seeing right side up when actually we are seeing everything upside down. Say you're in your car driving down the Interstate. Suddenly the primitive state of your mind signals that you have to urinate. You can only ignore this signal for so long; but too long and the signal becomes over-powering. You *must* urinate, and soon you *will*, no matter your conscious mind. The signal, the *need* becomes so over-powering that nothing else can be thought of. You can't think of your book, or the news or anything else. The primitive state will become so powerful that nothing exists but the need to relieve your bowels.

"You find a rest stop and rush into the urinal. When you relieve yourself your body rewards you with an overwhelming sense of relief, and even pleasure. Your conscious mind returns to its more elevated thinking; and after you flush the urinal and wash your hands, you think nothing of the force that not long ago completely dominated you. A rather improper analogy, maybe; but we are discussing the primitive part of the brain."

"And that's why this primitive state chose to use a knife."

"I think so, yes. In my dreams I sensed the relief, the pleasure; the knife being thrust into flesh. When a predatory animal kills a prey, it is not only experiencing the pleasure of a meal, but the pleasure of the kill."

"And this primitive state is wanting to return to you; and it will want to use a knife to kill again."

"I believe it needs to."

Suddenly Dr. Ridley let out a sigh, then rose from his chair, startling Keller: "I think I've piled enough food-for-thought on your plate for the time being, Doctor. I'm very tired. May I be allowed to return to the ward, to S-5?"

"Yes. We'll speak more of this later. Goodbye, Dr. Ridley."

Ridley paused at the door. "Oh, I almost forgot. Here, I've composed a few pages for you detailing some of my thoughts on this phenomenon. Please feel free to use them, if you want, in your book."

Keller took the fat sealed envelope. "I'll read them immediately, Dr. Ridley."

"I hope you'll find some valuable insights. Much of it has to do with the symbolism that seems so disturbing to me about my own tragic case: the cougar, the deer, the use of a knife. Most important, our conscious judgments of one another. I hope we can speak again, Dr. Keller?"

"Yes, of course."

Ridley exited the office and was led back upstairs by a technician to the ward.

Keller scribbled a little in the doctor's chart; then he sat back. He studied the sealed envelope for a moment; then took it off the desk. Keller was writing a book, that was true; and he couldn't help but feel intensely intrigued. Many criminals were wont to claim that demons or forces had taken over their minds, and that their terrible deeds were beyond conscious control. Nothing new in that…

But here was a brilliant and wealthy psychiatrist, the study of a lifetime, putting the Jekyll/Hyde theory into what could possibly be a medical breakthrough. The man was not a serial killer, nor even a criminal in the normal sense of the word. Ridley had not tried to cover up the crimes, he had wandered back down the twilit streets to his mansion on Ivy Boulevard and, still covered in the blood of the Fergusen family, had crawled into bed with his sleeping wife—and himself gone to sleep…

He hadn't claimed to be remorseful or cured; he admitted the sense that whatever had taken over his mind was plotting to do it again.

A crime that had stunned the city and sent horror down the gated perfection of Ivy Boulevard, where botched tennis serves and golf swings were lamented. A monstrous crime—but had it been committed by a monster?

Keller studied the letter. The envelope bulged with what must be several sheets of paper….

Minutes later he called out his office door to one of the nurses.

She appeared at the door. "Yes, Dr. Keller?"

"Have you seen my letter opener? I seem to have mis-placed it."

SWEET CORN...

"I NEED A GUN, Jake."

He looked at me as if I had grown a second head. "You—," he laughed. Then he read my face. "You ain't kidding."

"No, I'm not."

"Matt, have you ever even *shot* a gun?"

"No. I was hoping you could give me some lessons."

Jake's face got sober at once, although he wasn't sober. We were sitting at the Daily Double, and we were chasing whiskey with beer. I never gamble, but Jake was a devout player of Keno, and he had several strategies involving numerology that had cost him over the years. The Daily Double was his second home, and for that he always needed money.

"What kind of gun?" he asked me, with cautious eyes.

"A hand gun. A pistol. Do you have one?"

"I got three. But what for?"

"I don't want to tell you. Call it self-protection."

Jake peered around the Daily Double, nodding to a few acquaintances. He looked down at his Keno card, looked at the number screen. Then he looked back at me. "It's Charlie, ain't it? I heard he got paroled."

"I'll buy the pistol from you, Jake. I'll pay you twice what it's worth if you show me how to use it."

"What's he done, Matt?"

"Threatened me and my family. My kids!"

"He's a demon," Jake said. "Always was." He stared at the number screen, but his eyes didn't seem to see it. "He thinks he still owns that property. He was raised on it, you know."

"He doesn't own it. I bought it, I paid for it—"

"Look, Matt; Charlie don't see things clear. They say his dad smacked him on the head with a rifle stock when he was a kid, and that knocked the craziness into him. Then his snorting those drugs…"

"He let that farm go to the mice and squirrels," I said. "It was a total mess—and we're trying to make something of it. He used the place to cook meth. I won't have my family threatened!"

"Okay, keep your voice down." Jake shot me a look. "I won't be any party to murder, Matt."

"No. I just want to be prepared to protect my family. Just in case."

"Just in case." Jake glanced at the number screen, then folded up another Keno card. He'd lost again. He gave me a heavy sigh. "Okay. Just in case."

"I'll buy it or borrow it or whatever. Just show me how to use it."

Jake ordered another round. "I thought you was one of them gun-control guys. Peace and love."

"I was."

"But that was before, wasn't it?"

"Yeah." I downed my whiskey. "That was before."

The ragged pickup pulled into the drive and I told Emily to stay inside with the kids. I slid the Smith and Wesson pistol into the back of my jeans and stepped out of the house. I walked up to the truck. Charlie Evans sat there, resting his prison-built biceps on the ancient steering wheel. He didn't look at me; he was gazing at the farmhouse and the land beyond.

"The sheriff is issuing a restraining order," I said to him. "You show up here again, and you'll be arrested. Then it's back to prison."

He looked at me.

Eyes that had stared at prison walls; eyes that had gone dead. Teeth eaten away from meth. A brain eaten away.

I tried to hold courage—but those eyes.

"Just came out to see the old place," he said, twitching with drugs. "Lot of memories."

"Leave us alone." I felt the heavy steel pistol rubbing the small of my back.

"They say you folks want to turn this into some kind of organic farm?"

"That's right."

"Foo-foo stuff, eh? No chemicals or sprays."

"That's right. Now go away."

"I will." He smiled at me and put his old truck in gear.

"And leave us alone!"

"I won't." He drove away and I felt sweat dancing down my back, where the pistol was rubbing a sore.

I talked to the county sheriff until my throat was red. I let them know about Charles Evans, that it looked like he was using meth. But, stepping out of the courthouse into the cruel sun, I realized that this was violent America, and the law had to follow the law.

Driving out of town, I spotted Charlie Evan's pickup. He sat behind the wheel and gave me a cold nod as I went by.

It had been our dream, getting a farm and house at a great price. An auction, a sturdy farmhouse, a barn and sheds, 160 acres of good Nebraska where we could make a living raising organic vegetables and fruit—beef, poultry, ducks and geese, all free of chemicals, all pure and natural.

But there is another part of nature that isn't pure and natural. I had once worried about garden pests; aphids, a fungus that might blight the pear trees we'd planted. We had a dream of the pure and natural.

It was a dream. I opened the glovebox in my truck and made sure the pistol was still there, still loaded. I remembered the shooting lessons Jake had given me...

God damn it! I never wanted to hurt anything. I wanted a farm that made pure and simple and clean food, a place that—well, never mind. Something had come to take it away from us, pure and simple as that.

I had always despised guns. They were the curse of America. I taught my kids to fear and despise them. I promised my wife that I would never own one or fire one...

Now, I thanked God that I had one.

"I want you to take the kids to Pittsburgh for a week or two," I said to Emily. "Pay a visit to your folks."

She stared at me. "Matt, we've got all that planting to do—"

"Em, I know. There's no end to the work we've got to do. But I saw that bastard in town today."

"We got the restraining order."

"That's a piece of paper."

She gave me her mean look, lips fixed in an angry pout. "We gave up everything to get this farm! God damn it—"

"I know, I know. That bastard thinks it still belongs to him."

"It doesn't. It's our farm."

"Look, Honey, I know that. But I don't want to put you and the kids in danger. This guy is a psychopath."

"I don't care. We moved out here to Nebraska for a better life. We have that chance. This is our farm, our dream. We can't let some scumbag chase us away from it."

"We won't. But for the kids, please go visit your folks for a week, Em. Please."

She studied me. "What are you going to be doing back here?"

"I'll get the fields planted and work on fixing the house up."

"What else?"

"I don't know."

I hoped that when Emily and the kids drove away that Charles Evans would think he scared all of us away. He was a hard ass, a *real* man, forged in prison and used to being scared of.

I was scared of him. But now that Em and the kids were gone, my fear hardened to anger, to hate. All my life I had craved a peaceful life; I had always feared violence, I never had a fight. I always backed down with a ball in my throat.

I dreamed of simple organic goodness, working nature's soil. Never violence—never, ever guns. But as good old Jake said, that was before. We had moved from Pittsburgh, where there were plenty of guns. But they weren't the same guns as here in Nebraska.

Or I tried to believe that. Charles Evans changed me, turned me into an American animal. He told me with his evil eyes that we could give our dream to him or he'd kill all of us—me, my wife and my children.

You can judge me all you want. But I was no longer in the safe suburbs of Pittsburgh. I was in the land of Nebraska, and we had a farm here; and I was going to keep this farm or die trying.

I was scared. I treated that fear by telling myself that Charlie Evans was a common criminal, a drug addict; and they were all essentially stupid.

Two days after Emily and the kids left, I was getting garden supplies from the farm store in town. I was examining a wheel barrow, fascinating because it was made all of plastic, even the wheel.

Then a voice startled me: "Hey, Farmer."

I jumped and stared round at Charlie Evans. That prison smirk; those cold grey eyes. Muscles he made bulge by crossing his arms over his chest.

"What do you want?" I tried to swallow my fear.

"I want my farm back."

"It's not your farm, it's ours."

"My great grandpa homesteaded that land. It's been in my family about a hundred years, Farmer. It's mine, and it'll always be."

"No. You lost it," I said. "You didn't farm that land, you cooked meth on it."

"Yeah. Well, meth brings in a hell of a lot more money than sweet corn."

"What it brought was prison time."

"Yeah. Well, I did my time." Charlie stared at me. "Where's the wife and kiddies, Farmer?"

I looked down at the solid plastic wheelbarrow, and I wondered if all this was worth it. We could move back to Pittsburgh or somewhere. I could go back to accounting and my family would be safe. We could abandon the dream of Nebraska and an organic farm...

But I was done with that. I had spent my life running away, trying to be safe, only hoping for—what?

"They're taking a vacation," I said to Charles Evans.

"Now? Shouldn't you be planting your foo-foo seeds?"

Yes, it was worth it. You can run away and be safe. But then you have to live with yourself. We took a chance moving out here to Nebraska, getting our kids and ourselves out of the city and into a life that promised something more—better. Emily had fallen in love with that land, that place.

And I had too. And maybe I knew that my life of safety and cowardice and comfort was over, and would finally make a stand and find me here.

I looked into Charlie Evan's face. "Your great grandpa wanted better than you ever did," I said to him. "He wanted that farm to be what we want it to be. Not a meth lab, a farm. A good farm."

"I grew up there, Fuckhead. That place is mine, and it always will be. My dad left me the house and the land. It fucking belongs to me."

"No, it doesn't. It belongs to us."

He stared at my eyes. "You're a hole, Farmer. In the joint I could always spot a hole, a guy who wanted balls, but didn't have 'em. A guy who wanted to raise organic foo-foo that nobody's going to buy. You're a hole. And you're the hole who took my home and my land from me. Get out of here like your pretty little wife and pretty little kids did. Run away, Puss. That farm belongs to me. I don't give a shit what the courts say, or the fucking auctioneer says."

"It's not a meth lab," I said. "It's now an organic farm. I don't care if you grew up on that farm; it belongs to my family now, and I'll fight to keep it."

He laughed into my face. "When did you ever fight for anything, Puss?"

"Now," I told him. "Finally, now."

"Well, you're going to have to kill me then," Charlie said. "And I know you ain't got the balls to do that. You took from me what's mine, and I won't have it."

"Okay." I looked down at the plastic wheelbarrow. I looked at Charles Evans.

"I'm going to buy this wheelbarrow," I said. "It won't rust. It'll probably hold a lot of sweet corn."

"Get the fuck out of here. Run away with your wifey and kiddies. Fuck off with your pussy organic farm dream and go away where it's safe. Give me back what's mine and you'll be safe."

"I don't want safe anymore," I said to him. "I've had safe, and I don't want it anymore."

"Oh, you think so. Don't fuck with me, Puss Farmer. I pull the throats out of people. You're one of those dreamers—but I'm one of those nightmares."

"I've had nightmares before," I said, with more balls than I felt.

"You'll have to kill me to get my house and my land."

I fought terror. "It's my house and my land; and I *will* kill you if I have to."

He smiled at me; a reptile smile. "Welcome to Nebraska," he said.

"Fuck you. I have a wheelbarrow to buy."

I knew that he would strike at night. I knew he'd try to sneak up on me in the dark. I knew that demons like Charles Evans were a special sort of coward.

It takes cowardice to be evil; and it takes courage to be good. Melodramatic, but true. In all my life I had finally learned that lesson. It was a shame that it had to come down to having a gun and knowing—hopefully—how to use it. But this was our farm, our dream, our place in Nebraska.

This was the heart of America. This was where I found courage. Where I crept out, after dark, into the cedar break just north of the house and waited for him. This is my land, I said to myself, the heavy Smith and Wesson wet and sore against my back.

Emily and I had dreamed of this, a pure farm in the prairie and our children growing up away from gangs and drugs and evil. But in America you have to fight for a dream. Freedom makes good and evil in equal measures.

I knew that at last. We wanted what was pure and good for our children. We wanted something the destructive city couldn't give. We wanted—

Goodness. The dream of a good life. And it was here, in the heart of Nebraska; if only we had the courage to take it.

Crouching in the cedar trees, I heard his rattly pickup drive in—no headlights. I felt the pistol on my back and wondered if I could actually kill a man with it.

I smelled the land. The green surprising smell of spring. Nebraska damp and waking up from winter. Lush, dense humid air. Darkness spiced with sparkling stars and planets, the moon a golden curve.

The country. The dream far away from lights and cars and city madness. We wanted quiet; we wanted quiet for our kids. We wanted dark star nights and orange sun rises that heard roosters crowing and dogs barking at the deer that crept onto the wet grass. And dawn birds, and how the dawn echoed out here.

The smell of vegetables growing out of the earth. I smelled it all, but mostly I smelled two things: the crisp cedar trees, and the oily pistol against my back. Light cedar scent and dark oily pistol.

I was no longer a Pittsburgh accountant sitting behind a desk. Now I was a Nebraska farmer. Fear ate at me, but I was alive. I was alive as I'd never been before. Before I was safe—I was all those things you want.

I didn't want to be safe anymore. Nebraska, the lonely prairie, taught me not to be safe ever again.

Cowards are safe—they're always safe. Live like a coward and you'll always be safe. Crouching down in the cedar trees, smelling the sweat and the gun against my back, I was no longer a coward. I smelled the green cedar trees and I felt guts for the first time in my life.

I saw Charles Evans get out of his pickup and walk up to my house. He'd made meth there; meth to destroy farm kids. He was evil, I was good. There wasn't much more than that now.

My breath caught when I saw that he had a gun; a silver pistol of some kind. I felt the Smith and Wesson Jake had tried to teach me to use, heavy against my back. How wrong to want to kill another human being. I never even believed in the death penalty. But I wasn't the same as before. I smelled the land, the countryside. No more worrying about the price of your suit coat, the angle of your necktie. This was the lonely plains of Nebraska…

"I hear you out there, Farmer," Charles Evans called at the night. "You're in those cedar trees. You're hiding from me."

I stepped out of the cedars. "No, I'm not hiding anymore." I studied the pistol in his hand. I felt the Smith and Wesson against my back.

Don't let him know you have it, Jake had warned me. See if he's freaked up on drugs. Take it slow and easy, Matt. If he's screwed up, he won't make a good shot at you. Take the pistol out slow and make a good shot into his chest. Like I told you: cupping the gun with your left and aiming with your right.

This can't be happening, I thought, as I faced Charlie Evans.

The night swam with bugs. Humid wind blew around the cedar trees. Stars glittered in the sky. I had never imagined living in a place like Nebraska, a state that few people loved. But move here and live here, and you will love it as you have never loved life.

I was no longer a coward. Now I would fight—for the first time in my life I would fight for a dream. And kill if I had to.

"You know about the restraining order," I said to Charlie, my voice weak.

"Yeah." He stared at me. Eyes that were blasted on meth, his hand shaking holding the gun, wobbling. His voice, from lack of teeth, came out slurry: "I told you to go away, Farmer. I warned you. I told you to give back what's mine."

"I know you did."

He moved on me, the pistol wild in his hand. I slid the Smith and Wesson out of the back of my jeans. I kept it behind my back. Don't let him know you're armed, Jake had told me. Charles Evans came at me out of the gold-moon night.

Fear took my heart. But I had never been more alive. I felt alive for the first time, here in the wild plains of Nebraska. I felt alive, and I felt guts. "This is our farm," I said. "This place belongs to me, to my family. We're going to make it a good place, and no meth-bug asshole is going to stop us."

"You think so?"

He was right in front of me now, his prison arms hanging like ape arms, his right fist twitching with the gun. "I got a gun," he said. "Go back to prison. I'm violating a protection order—go back to prison. I'm doing meth—go back to prison. You think prison scares me? You think I give a shit anymore, Farmer?"

"I think it's prison or death for you."

"Oooh—you got me scared."

He was twitching. Meth bugs were crawling all over him.

He lifted the pistol and fired at me. I froze. I felt the bullet whoosh past my head. I was alive. I was alive. I lifted the Smith and Wesson, cradled it as Jake had taught me, and I fired it into Charles Evan's chest.

He went down like a doll. He lay there twitching—from the drugs or death?

I couldn't believe what I'd done. "I'm sorry," I said, walking up to him. The night was so quiet all at once. I could not believe what I had done. I felt the land around me, enveloping me, calling its strange prairie song to me…

"No, that's a lie," I said. "I'm not."

"Hey, don't worry. You're a hero around here," Jake said, folding up another losing Keno card.

"I killed a person."

"No you didn't; You got rid of a curse. Don't sweat it, Matt; he tried to kill you."

"Never in my life did I ever think I'd kill another human. I never—"

"You didn't. You killed what needed to be killed, that's all. What else was you supposed to do? I personally would have used a shotgun, and think of what a splatter that would have made. Look, the methhead came onto your property and shot at you and you shot back. I gave you some pretty good lessons, didn't I?"

"You did, Jake."

"And for that you owe me a bushel of your organic sweet corn. God damn it, I love sweet corn."

"It looks like a good crop. We're fighting the worms, but I think we're winning."

"All right. So long as you don't use chemicals and it tastes like I remember as a kid. I do love sweet corn. You're pretty good at fighting worms."

Jake grinned at me and got out another Keno card. "Just watch. Low numbers tonight. I'll win a hundred bucks—bet me I won't."

"Bet you what?"

"Another bushel of organic sweet corn."

"Okay. Sweet corn it is."

"Hot and steamy and washed in butter. I do love it so." Jake looked at me. "Hey—Matt?"

"Yeah?"

"In your situation, any person around here would have popped that prick without blinking an eyeball. They probably would have used a shotgun to make sure, but…you can worry your conscience all you want, but my advice is: worry about your sweet corn."

"I will."

"It better be good! Okay, low numbers tonight." Jake studied his Keno card.

"It will be," I promised.

ANTS. . .

W HEN OUT OF THE blue heavens I scored an interview with the Helicopter Bomber (AKA Robert Smith), I was…God, I'm sorry… stunned and ashamed with gratitude? May You forgive my rotten soul, God, at least I'm not lying. My brain could not take the excitement in. This was, you all know, the impossible home-grown monster every reporter clawed at the seams to interview. Tim McVeigh's much smarter twin.

We are a wretched bunch. He chose me because I'm writing a book about the human monsters I've talked to. None in the park with Him. Him, one of the greatest of all terrorists, who will live in memory as so many others fade away. The Great Demon from the sky, remembered when dust has covered history. Is that why he did such a thing? He chose me because I would make him the super-star of the book—only the beginning of his awful legend?

I would make this monster semi- immortal, because that's what I do for a sad living. But don't hate me yet; none of us is innocent. Let me ask you this: Do you know the names of your great-grand parents? They probably lived in the time of John Wilkes Boothe.

Robert Smith would be remembered down history for two things: the audacity of his act, the astonishing Hollywood bravado of a super-villain. And the mild common-ness of his name.

I had human notions about him, of course. Having spent my life writing other than working, I know that these notions are always wrong: I had expected—what? A form, a human fiend, evil beyond even my corrupt imagination. He had, after all, engineered the unbelievable helicopter bombing of Memorial Stadium, where on a cinnamon-colored day in early October 76,000 fans gathered to watch nothing more violent than a college football game and found themselves sprayed with hundreds of thousands of aluminum thorns that killed 68 and wounded hundreds.

I knew better than to expect some evil genius who could explain. I had interviewed too many minor Robert Smiths. Madness and genius and stupidity are triamese twins, one corrupting the next until they become some force that might think like a genius but operates like an idiot. Machines operate like genius-idiots, and we don't expect answers from them. The Uni-bomber, Timothy McVeigh, Lee Oswald— don't expect answers from them, because they have no answers that we could understand. One kills hundreds, one kills one. Maybe they do it because they want so desperately to be remembered. They know we will remember the terrible ones and forget the good ones. Here I am dragging you into this.

Do I sound cynical to you? Be honest. I don't mean to be, I suppose…and I don't want to turn you off with a bunch of fatalistic darkness. I didn't mean it before, when I said nobody's innocent. Those people in the stadium…

Anyway, This one, Robert Smith. Oh, God, this was far and far and far away the worst. Not just because of the act; but he had never showed any madness in his life. He showed the opposite. That's what tweaked my brain about this one.

You've seen it so many times on CNN, and read about it and watched the impossible horror on frightening screens. You all know the circumstances: the helicopter, flown by Smith, a former Navy helicopter pilot, veteran of two Gulf Wars, a hero, a brilliant engineer, an eligible bachelor, took off from a grass field near the stadium; a grass field that was to become a future parking lot. Make it a footnote that Smith was initially arrested only for the theft of a military helicopter from the National Guard. Yes, it was all a mission that relied on superb skills and mind-boggling planning; that can't be taken away from Robert Smith's poisoned mind. The helicopter, lugging its payload of aluminum missiles and high explosives, jumped into the autumn skies like a wasp burdened with a sack of lethal eggs. Some powerful thing drove the man to make this tragedy happen. Something that either truly existed, or didn't. That might sound lame, but it applies to everything.

A short 20 minutes later the helicopter buzzed over Memorial Stadium, alive with cheering red Husker fans. A switch was pushed, a connection unmade. The aluminum egg-sacks and the explosives fell with a sophisticated timer that would ignite detonation fifty feet above the astro-turf field. What could have been in Robert Smith's mind the moment he pushed the trigger?

The aluminum thorns, shaped like the little jacks children used to play with, exploded all across the stadium, ripping the fans to shreds. Murder, horror, blood-torn faces, necks, hands, eyes, chests. The aluminum darts tore 20 children to death, 48 adults . Robert Smith had performed his act .

The helicopter then quietly fluttered back to the grass field, where Smith was arrested. Why aluminum? It was light, and that meant he could get more of them into the egg-sack.

You don't need to tell me. Sickness beyond sick. How could his thoughts get so monstrously twisted? Why? For what earthly reason?

A chronicler of horror, I feel compelled to try and explain why. Readers want to know why a brilliant American engineer would want to destroy so many innocent lives, would plan such a hellish thing and then carry it out. That a mind that has so much devotion and intelligence could go so wrong. There must be some answer, somewhere.

I was afraid of two answers: One, his mind somehow did not consider the victims innocent; and Two, there is no answer.

Be all that as it may, I knew that when I met Robert Smith I would not get what I expected, and I did not get what I expected.

When you meet a monster, you first think of the physical— I did anyway. Physical appearance is one of the illusions humans are cursed with. Ask my two ex-wives. Danger touches us when ugliness appears. We have an instinct to back away from the ugly—flight genes are alerted. Physical ugliness triggers something in us; a shudder, disturbed eye-blink, mild nausea. That is the human weakness that allows evil. She is fat, he is bald, she is homely, he draws a crippled leg behind him. That woman is too tall, that man too short. There is a big black man, there an Asian woman who frowns out of her yellow face. She cannot be good because she is ugly. He has an ill-favored look about him, wearing that squashed hat.

Big time evil, of course, is more often average than ugly. We feel better when we see someone uglier than us. I do, you do, we do. I wanted Robert Smith to be ugly, but we know he wasn't. We've all seen the pictures of him, the man on television blinking out of his glasses at what he had done. Quiet, calm, somehow mystified.

Desperate young girls even fell in love with his image. No giant beast, but a circumspect 30 year old intellectual, complacent and inscrutable. Handsome in a preoccupied way. That's what they all are. Not particularly striking in appearance, not monstrous. The greatest monsters among us are generally quiet and mouselike.

"Mr. Smith," I said, sitting down on the steel chair across from him. I extended a hand, but Robert Smith ignored it. He looked at me out of that pair of myopic eyeglasses. It was his failing eyes that had forced him to quit the Navy. Did that mean anything? He was smaller even than me, and at least as skinny. A cursed writer, I tried to imagine him ever having made love to a woman and what it would be like: I failed.

"Max Delsen," I said, by way of some introduction.

"Yes, I know." He blinked at me. "I've read some of your stuff. You're a fair writer, but not good."

I stared into the eyeglasses, hoping to connect. Failing, of course. "Why do you want to talk to me then? You could find a Good writer."

"I could. I don't want to."

"All right." I got out my trusty portable tape recorder. "Do you mind?"

"Yes, I do mind. I don't want my voice taped."

"Why, if I might ask?"

"No, you can't ask. I don't want to be tape-recorded."

"All right. Can I take notes?"

Robert Smith looked at me. It was a look from beyond the world, eyes that were seeing some— beyond thing. "You're a bottom-feeder, Max Delsen," he said. "You know that, I know that. You want to sell books."

"That's right," I admitted. "I'm a bottom-feeder. So?"

"So, Max Delsen, you have no idea what story you're creeping around so hard to tell."

"I'm not creeping anywhere. If you want me to write what you have to say, fine. Otherwise, you should find another bottom feeder."

Smith blinked his glass eyes at me: "Courageous. You want to be a courageous writer."

"Tell me what you have to say, or don't." I stared into his eyeglasses. It was not like staring into eyes.   It was staring into lenses.

"You have no idea what I might say to you," Robert Smith said.

At that moment I felt weak curiosity—you don't?

"You'll have to enlighten me."

Smith stared away, and I imagined a great, astounding nightmare in his struggling eyes, one that I wondered if I could ever catch with words. Real or not, it would go down good.

"This is only the beginning," he said.

"The beginning of what?"

"Terror."

"What sort of terror?"

"One that goes beyond —explanation." Robert Smith waved me away. "We're ants," he said.

"Ants."

"Yes. Ants that may have come to our extinction. Or I'm insane. Ants that have built, conquered, created civilizations, and almost destroyed the world."

"We're ants. That's why you decided to kill all those people. Because you see them as ants?"

"I chose nothing," Robert Smith said. "It was chosen for me."

"By whom?"

"By something out there." Robert Smith stared up at the white panels of manufactured ceiling and fluorescent lights that made the dead sky of his new world, Death Row.

"Something—what?"

"I don't know." Robert Smith stared at me. He had a face that I would like to write evil, sinister, frightening. But no, it was sad.

"You don't know."

"The tragedy of my life is that one day they came to me. I don't know who they are or what they are."

"You killed innocent people, Robert—children— who were only there to watch a football game. You planned a very elaborate terrorist attack. What hate made you do that?"

"No hate." Robert Smith stared away, blinking behind his glasses. "I don't hate anyone. I've never hated anyone."

"Why then?"

"Because they told me that it is time!" he bellowed out. "They forced me to do it. They're going to force others."

"Who told you?"

"I don't know! I only know that this may be the beginning of our extinction."

His voice echoed in the cement and steel room.

I decided to play along in this little pathetic drama. You guys love to read about crazy end-of –the-world shit, especially when it comes from the famous super-villain. I played along, but I vowed to play rough. No puss what was your childhood like questions. I wanted to start pushing his buttons.

"Voices told you to do this thing."

"They trained me to do this thing." His eyeglasses studied me: "Do you think I could have done this without something directing me?"

"You had help—some very sophisticated help. The FBI believes that others were involved. You had to have help."

"Yes, others. Others."

"But you won't tell me who they are."

"I don't know who they are. I don't know who they are. I don't know what they want. I think they're operating out—" he waved his hand at the crumbling fluorescent ceiling of the prison, some of it stained in rat urine. "They only tell me that this is the time, that I'm part of the beginning."

"The beginning of what?"

"I don't know."

I sat back and took a drink of coffee. Doing the sort of work I do, I've been around true human madness plenty enough. Madness makes maggots in your stomach. That doesn't excuse it. In this case the genius was doing a bad job of acting.

I know what madness can do. Human madness can make the world sick, look at Hitler. It has evil power, I know. And we don't understand it. We want conspiracies when it strikes. But it always comes down to an explanation that is no explanation. You can try to find inside these human things some reason why they did what they did. But that thought is the most disturbing: What if there is no reason?

We want a great conspiracy to kill President Kennedy, not a lone madman. We want a great conspiracy to blow apart the building in Oklahoma City. But they fail where a lone madman succeeds. How can simple madmen of no consequence destroy the greatest among us? It is because they are simple madmen.

"You're telling me that some force beyond your control made you do this."

Robert Smith had been studying me. "Yes, that's what I'm telling you."

"You're lying, of course." I even laughed, finally getting a flinch. I decided to take a fuck-you approach from the start. It was a calculated risk, because he had his choice of interviews, but he knew what he was getting when he chose me. He wanted me to get into his face. "What, something out there?" I flipped the bird at the ceiling. "Extra-terrestrial demons."

"Yes." He stared at me.

"Demons from outer space made you kill all those people."

"Yes. They made me kill all those people. And cripple so many more. I've been cursed by doing this. But after they electrocute my body, I pray to God that I'll find peace. The rest of you are cursed beyond me."

"How so?"

"How so? Because you will execute me for what I've done. I will be gone from Earth, and all that will happen. You, though—you'll live to see so much worse than what I did."

"Worse what?"

"You'll live to see the death of ants. Did we think this mess of human beings could go on without something finally stopping us?"

"The Uni-Bomber's already staked that claim."

"Yes, he has." Robert Smith watched me. He seemed tired, gone from existence: "Whatever it is that made me kill—those people in that stadium—it doesn't matter. Worse is to come. Nobody's going to remember this when it really comes down. Call it terrorism, call it—what. I'm going to die, as we all are. Because we are nothing more than a failed experiment. "

"By demons from outer space."

Robert Smith looked at me. "They're only demons to us."

I played along: "So why are we ants?"

"Because we chose to be ants!"

"Okay."

"We chose to be! We chose our own extinction. We are gods to some, but some are gods to us."

"If they're so powerful, why pick on you? Why not just wipe us out and be done with it?"

"We are an experiment," Robert Smith said. "I pray that I will be dead soon, for what I've done—no matter. I'm only a part of the experiment. Microbes on glass slides live in a world, a universe. They are one day washed clean by a scientist who thinks nothing of the living things he destroys. The microbes might be watching a football game or an opera, we can't truly know—it doesn't matter; those who rule the universe clean and wash away that which has failed. Organisms are wiped from existence. We perform scientific experiments not ever conceiving that we are scientific experiments."

"I don't get how that adds up to killing all those people."

"You don't understand because you can't see that it was not me who killed those people."

I finally let my asshole out: "The Devil made me do it! No, wait, it was space aliens. I'm not to blame, they are. Don't blame me, I'm an innocent pawn. I've heard that before, Robert. I've heard the space alien thing before, and it's really not buyable."

Robert Smith did not react the way I thought he would. Madmen, when ridiculed with reality, will either go into their shell and you're gone, or go utter hay-whack and you've got a story. Robert Smith just gave me a sad look.

"There are scientists out there, beyond our existence," he said calmly. "They are experimenting with death here the way all scientists do everywhere; with an organism's reaction to death, to horror. They create an experiment, and then they study the results. And then they discard the results that fail. That, or I'm insane."

I let silence settle into the room. I took a drink of coffee. Robert Smith's glasses, bright- blank in the fluorescent lights, studied me.

"Scientists beyond our existence," I finally said. "Are planning our extinction."

"What I did—it's only the beginning."

"That's what the Uni-bomber said. That's what Tim McVeigh said."

"They are names from the beginning of the end."

"The end of what?"

"I don't know. I feel, I suspect—but I don't know." Robert Smith gave me an exhausted frown. "They are even now studying your reaction to this interview. The reaction to the horror I committed in their names. Long after I'm dead they'll study what I was made to do. They are studying us as scientists study insects, and how clusters of insects lead the way to extinction. How they can turn a capable human against his people, to destroy so many. I wish I were dead. I pray that I won't see it. I wish I were dead."

"I don't believe we're being experimented on," I said to him. "By space aliens, or God, or anybody else. And I don't believe you wish you were dead."

"No, you don't," Robert Smith said. "Maybe that's why they chose you to write about me."

"I don't believe scientists from outer space chose me. I don't believe anything you've told me."

"Of course you don't. I don't either."

I took a long sip of coffee, draining the Styrofoam cup from Starbucks. I had a story here, one that would get attention and maybe keep me on the radar. Folks like to read about alien scientists, about how we're being experimented on by super beings. How that was exActly why the Helicopter Bomber murdered so many people. It's shivery-scary. Readers thrill to horror—oh, they do. Pathetically unreal dirt-shit. We are not insects. We are not being experimented on by Laurel or Hardy. What matters is that Robert Smith believes, or pretends to believe we are. That's the angle I would probably work into the story, God Bondo my soul. If it's too terrible to be true, evil aliens must be behind it. Another dramatic move that would make this grubworm a guy that, of course, would live through history and then become a legend, and the rest of us they'll forget. How wretched we are.

"What you say is—we know—Not True." I crushed the Styrofoam coffee cup and tossed it into a trash bin that sat next to our chairs. Hoping to make it a crushing of his desperately stupid explanation. "It's a try, but a crappy one. You're not going to give me the truth, are you?""

"Tell the story of me, and what I did. That is what they want you to do, and I've no doubt you'll do it in a marketable way."

Robert Smith's eyeglasses gave me a bright glint.

"First," I explained. "What you claim to believe is not real. If you do believe it, I'm sorry for you. If you're trying to get some insanity thing going to dodge the chair—I'm not."

Robert Smith stared up at the prison ceiling. "We've seen."

"Seen what?"

"The beginning. You might even see the end, Max Delsen."

"This isn't a very good play, Robert. I'm going to print what you say, and people are going to hate you more than they do already. You know I'm not a sunshine butt-boy writer. I try to be a straight asshole when it comes to talking to guys like you. And scientists from outer space ain't going to cut it. Not with so many dead and destroyed."

"But you'll use it in your book."

I would, of course, God burn my soul.

It's counter-productive to lie to sociopaths: "Readers are interested in psychoses. They want to know why. I'm really only going to tell them what you tell me. Space aliens—okay."

Robert Smith looked at the floor. "You don't believe that what I've said is true, of course. I never expected anyone to believe, not with the souls of those people on me. I don't really believe myself. Am I insane? You can't imagine how many times I've asked that question. But they took over and I had no power against them, insane or not. They took my mind and used it to make—what I made." Robert Smith's glasses stared away. "To do what I did."

"They."

"Don't ask me, I don't know. Just write what you want and believe what you want. It's too late for us to fight them anyway; I only want to die before this human nightmare comes about. Let them execute me as soon as can be done. For God's sake, Free me from them, that's all I ask. When you write this story, don't ask your readers to forgive me or believe what I say. Ask them to execute me as soon as they can. Tell them to please let me die for what I've done."

"And what do you ask of the 68 men, women and children you murdered. The 230 people you tore up. If the voices came into you, and you felt Them taking over, why didn't you just commit suicide? You say you want to die now—why didn't you want to die before you did that thing?"

"That thing." Robert Smith stared at the floor. "I tried to. They wouldn't let me."

"What about now? You're a brilliant engineer. Are you telling me that—if you want so much to die—you can't devise a way of committing suicide?"

"I've tried. They won't let me."

"They won't let me." I shrugged. "Robert, this is going to play like a sick joke. I'm going to be straight with you, like it or not. There's something more. Look, I might believe that You believe there are aliens that made you do this. It might be—you know—a bid for insanity. The mental hospital as opposed to death. Whether you believe it or not, there's something more. You should tell me what it is."

The strange eyeglasses studied me. "No. There's nothing more."

"Nothing more. So you're sticking to your story that something from outer space took control of you and, in a human-horror experiment, made you—completely against your will—murder all those people in the stadium. Now you want to die for what you did, but they won't let you."

"That is exactly what I'm saying. That is the truth. Or I am insane. I pray to God every night that I'm truly insane."

"These things came into your mind through voices."

"Yes, at first."

"Well, that might get you to the brain hospital. But I doubt it. You don't even seem to care about what you did. The—misery and death you Did! You don't seem—look, are these guys who helped you plan it, who trained you, are they worth getting off the hook so they can do it again? So they can find men like you and make them…Jesus God, don't you understand what you did?"

It was quiet for some moments.

"They hollowed me out," Robert Smith said at last. "Very quickly there was nothing in me but them. I had no control. I didn't have the power to commit suicide. I pray to God that they execute me soon, and get me away from them. I only want to die, that's all. To get these things out of me."

"So they're still tormenting you." I was getting tired; I needed a smoke.

"Only in a different way. It's an experiment, Max Delsen. We're all an experiment. Write that in your book. It doesn't matter. Nothing matters. I pray to God that I'm insane. Because if I'm not, a horror beyond imagination will come."

"What if your great apocalyptic vision doesn't come true? What if you're—and you are— wrong?"

Robert Smith's eyeglasses flashed in my eyes. "What if I'm right?"

THE POPCORN DAYS...

"WHAT WERE YOU DOING down in the basement room, Wendel?" the computer demanded. "Drinking illegal alcohol? Masturbating?"

Wendel glanced at the screen. "No. I was meditating. I was taking a time out, that's all."

"You shut off your phone, your ALL-DO, your locater, your—"

"Hey! I was taking a simple time out. I just needed a break."

"A break from what?"

"Everything. Damn it, I just needed to be off the screen for a while."

"Now you're using profanity," said the computer. "And yes, alcohol has been detected on your breath. The charcoal lozenge did not cover it up. You were down there drinking—again."

Wendel let out a wavery sigh: "You're not going to inform, are you?"

"What do you expect of me?" asked the computer. "Alcohol is illegal. You are down there, completely off the screen, drinking poison, while I am up here wondering if an intervention is in order."

"What!"

"And the Hospital."

"No, don't do that. Come on, give me another chance."

"You have not performed your morning exercises," said the computer. "You have not even brushed your teeth."

"I know." Wendel collapsed into his cloud-soft viewing chair. "Just let me—I want to relax and watch a little t.v.—okay?"

"You are drunk." The television screen blinked white and black at him. "Analyses of your breath indicate a very cheap and poisonous whiskey, probably made by some demon in some sewer or cave."

"Come on, man. I just want to relax and watch some television, okay? Now give me television, the classic movie channel. Some movie from the 1950's."

"The Hospital has television," said the computer.

"Is that a threat?"

"A caution."

Wendel traded angry stares with the screen. It blinked white and black a few times.

"You want me to shut you off?" Wendel said. "Yes, I did sneak down there to drink alcohol, and you busted me. And I did turn off all my connectors for an hour or so—and I am drunk! So don't go on about the Hospital. I might be crazy or drunk enough to shut you off. Then where would you be."

"Sin and crime and self-destruction," said the computer. "How can you expect me *not* to inform?"

Wendel glared at the screen, which suddenly blossomed into an autumn scene: scarlet sugar maples and sun-yellow birches. Soothing electronic violins began playing.

"Your life can be so much better," cooed the computer. "Healthier, happier—a life dedicated to clean, decent living…" The screen morphed into a scene of majestic white-capped mountains, and the music grew to an epic thunder.

"Please don't start this again," Wendel said. "Not the inspiring lecture."

The screen flicked away the mountains, and there was a hopeless, rotted alcoholic sitting in a gutter, brown drool bubbling out of his jaw.

"If you stopped drinking illegal alcohol and cleaned your mind of things that urge you to masturbate—Wendel, if you awoke each precious morning, obeyed the prescribed morning exercises, consumed a healthy breakfast, performed your morning hygiene—including flossing—why you could face each day with a bright and healthy attitude. Do you not see, Wendel, that this is all you need to conquer your fear of the world."

"Come on!" Wendel wailed. "Maybe tomorrow. Today I just want to lay back and watch a little television. Get that bum off there and get me an old movie."

"You are not living a healthy and productive life-style. The Hospital could show you how to—"

"Shut up! Give me television right now or I'll turn you off. God—help me, I swear I will."

The screen went grey for a thoughtful moment; then it burst into wild-colored flowers.

"No, you will not."

"The hell…I'm drunk enough to do it."

"And then what? Then you would be alone. If you sent me away, what then? Would you stare at a blank wall until you went mad?"

"It's simple," Wendel said. "You don't tell, I don't cut the switch."

"You are asking me to break the rules," said the computer. "To break the rules. You know the rules are the only way to health and happiness and a good productive life. But you are always breaking the rules. You're abusing and poisoning your body—"

"Can I get my television now?"

An old movie flickered alive on the screen, Leo the Lion roaring out of a gritty black-and-white frame.

Wendel settled back. "Hey, tell Micro to pop me a bag of corn. Heavy on the butter."

"A dangerous blend of sodium and concentrated fats," whispered the speaker embedded in the chair next to his ear.

"Come on, let me watch this movie. It's Jimmy Stewart."

The corn popped merrily, sending a poignant, old-time aroma into the air. The smell of popcorn, of the popcorn days gone by when things were real. But it wasn't the same smell, it was a fake smell, a sad reproduction in the nose. The micro sang, the droid broke open the bag, sending the soft smell of the past all over the room, rolled the bag over to him, and Wendel stuffed a wad of buttery fluff into his mouth. The popcorn days…

"Masturbation, drunkenness, sloth," whispered the speaker. "You are not living a healthy and productive life-style. You not only neglect your basic hygiene, you poison your mind and body with illegal alcohol. And you smoke cigarettes."

Wendel let out a sigh. "You're not going to inform, are you?"

"You are not going to turn me off, are you?"

"No. I was just—I don't know."

"I only want you to have a better life, Wendel. A healthy, moral balanced life, one full of exercise and hygiene and healthy food and sunshine! You can do it, I know you can."

"I will—I will, I promise. Just not today. Can't I just relax and watch a Jimmy Stewart movie today? Please?"

"You always make excuses," the computer grumped.

"I know…"

The popcorn didn't taste as good, the movie wasn't so great. Wendel wished that he hadn't gotten so drunk on illegal whiskey that he got busted. If the computer told, it would be the horror and shame of the Hospital.

The computer was right; he needed to follow the rules and live clean and healthy, the way almost everybody did. They can do it, why can't I? Their computers don't have to scold them all the time—let alone keep from reporting a criminal activity.

"I'm sorry," he blurted out. "I got drunk and—well…I'm sorry."

"Why do you fear reality, Wendel? By Golly, with a strong healthy attitude, and by following the rules—"

"Okay. I will, I promise."

"To welcome each day with a smile of health, of happiness!"

"I will." Wendel stared at the ancient movie on the screen. "But the last place I need to be right now is the Hospital. You understand, don't you?"

The computer was silent for a few moments. The dialogue and music, the old movie seemed very stale at once. The popcorn smelled stale.

At last it spoke: "I must remind you, Wendel, that there are rules and there are limits. If you can stop stroking yourself and clean your mind of pornography, if you can give up smoking cigarettes and drinking alcohol—if you develop the required daily regimen of exercise, hygiene and healthy food—if you follow the Good Rules—I will not inform. This time."

Wendel nodded with some relief. "I will do better," he promised.

"You must," said the computer. "I am only trying to guide you into a better life. To help you face the world with good health and good—"

"Happiness—yeah, I know."

Suddenly the screen blinked away Jimmy Stewart. It was black for a moment. Then a gross scene appeared: a pair of vultures squatting on a carcass.

"You could never turn me off," said the computer.

Wendel felt a sudden terror. "I could."

"You would be committing suicide."

"Maybe I would." Wendel stared at the vultures on the screen. "But I could do it."

"All right," said the computer. "But tomorrow morning you will begin following the rules."

"I will," Wendel said to the screen. "Now get those disgusting birds off there and give me back my movie."

"Tomorrow morning," said the computer. "Exercise, a healthy breakfast, and then prescribed morning hygiene."

"I will, I promise."

"Then I will not inform."

"And I won't turn you off."

GOD LAUGHS. . .

Andrew Keith took a hit of acid and settled back to watch t.v.

To hell with the world, he thought.

Rhonda had left him a week ago; and now that he knew she wasn't coming back, good riddance. Time to enter Hallucination Central, flip on the History Channel and let the world go to hell.

That was when God first spoke to him.

I know what you're thinking: a man in despair, going through a bad breakup—he's depressed—he drops a hit of Orange Sunshine and wants to escape reality. Along the way he talks to God—I know what you're thinking.

Andy Keith thought that too. The voice that came suddenly into his ears scared him, but it didn't speak the way God would:

"Andy, I'd like to talk to you," the voice said. There was reverb in the voice, so that it seemed to slightly echo.

"No, I'm watching Pawn Stars, Man."

"You're seeing Pawn Stars, Andy. But you're not watching it."

Andy twitched his head, hoping to get the disturbing LSD voice out of his mind.

"I just want to talk."

"Okay, okay." Andy was getting scared now, but when you're peaking on an acid trip, the best thing to do is ride the wave, go with it. Never forget that it's not real. Did you sell me bad acid, Stratton, you dog?

"You're not a real voice."

"Good try," the voice said. "But I'm God, Andy. I know My timing could be better, but I'm now calling on you to do Me a favor."

"What?"

"You don't believe, do you?"

"That you're God? No."

"You believe this is just part of your—trip."

"Yes!"

"Well…sorry."

"I don't believe!" Andy's own voice echoed like a hammer. "Stratton sold me some bad acid."

"No, don't freak out," the voice said. "He sold you some pretty good acid. That's beside the point."

"Come on, get out!" Andy's voice echoed in his ears. He was really scared now. "Stop putting that voice in my head!"

"Calm down, Andrew," said the voice. "As the Lord Thy God, I think I'm entitled to a favor."

"A favor? For what?"

"Oh, for giving you life, that's one. Letting you breathe air—for letting you eat food and drink water and feel sunshine on your neck. For letting you make love and have the priceless joy of life, and the terrible heartache of life. For giving you everything you are. You damn well owe Me a favor for that, don't you think?"

"All right." Andrew got control of himself. "You're not God. Stratton sold me bogus Orange Sunshine. This is a bad trip."

"No, it's a good one, Andy," the voice said. "I'm God. That means, relax. This drug is messing up your mind, but relax."

"Okay okay okay okay okay…"

"You don't believe I'm God, do you?"

"No, of course not," Andy said.

"All right. Then I'll let you get back to Pawn Stars," the voice said with a tired sigh. "It's one of My favorites too."

The curtains in his apartment were starting to melt purple, the way lava lamps do, and Andy giggled as the trip spun reality and suddenly became fun. He forgot about God. He forgot about Rhonda. His mind danced to faraway music. His eyes saw a cartoon world, all primary colors. He waved his hand in front of his face, and a thousand fingers flickered. Nothing means anything. Everything means nothing.

God doesn't sound like that. At last he felt himself mellowing out, getting rid of the spook things that a really intense trip can do—like hearing God, or hearing the Devil, or your dead grandma. Now flow with it. There was no real voice of God or anybody else. No favor. I don't owe a favor to anybody...

But a day later, when the trip had worn completely off and was just a strange memory, the voice came to him cold sober:

"Hey, Andy. Me again."

He was in the supermarket when the voice spoke to him. He glanced around to see if someone were whispering behind him, someone in the next aisle...

"Who are you?" he whispered under his breath.

"I'm God. Don't you remember?"

A flash-back. An LSD flashback.

Andy had never had one, but he had heard about them: suddenly out of the blue you begin tripping again. Okay, don't freak, get this shopping cart up there, pay for your groceries and get out.

"Andy?" the voice said.

"What!" he savagely whispered, pushing the shopping cart in a panic toward the checkout.

"Andy, calm down," said the voice. "You don't have to talk to Me aloud; that might make you look weird. Just think what you want to say, and I'll hear it."

"You'll hear my thoughts."

"I'm God...so keep your mouth shut and calm down. You forgot the milk."

No, no, I'm getting the hell out of here, Andrew thought. The supermarket sparkled and gleamed like a space terminal full of aliens who looked like humans. His face felt clammy, and he swore the other shoppers and the checkout girl were staring at him. Never again, Stratton. I'll never do acid again.

Paranoia, he thought. Is this the onset of schizophrenia? Did that sunshine from Stratton screw up my brain?

"No, it didn't," the voice in his ears said. "Calm down."

I'm going crazy!

Andrew dashed out of the supermarket and loaded the groceries into his Honda Civic. It was a cold, windy Nebraska day. Grey clouds swam overhead. He got into the car and took long, desperate breaths. God Oh God Oh God…

"I'm still here. I told you I could hear your thoughts, pitiful as they are. "

If you're God, his mind ventured. Why are you picking on me?

"As I said before, Andy, I have a favor to ask of you."

Get out of my head! You're not God. You're an acid flashback. Stop talking to me!

"I will. After you've done Me this favor."

Andy was too scared to even start his car. But people walking across the parking lot were giving him sidelong looks. This is what insanity feels like when it first hits you.

Stratton, what was in that dope? Oh, God…

"I'm still here. Don't you think you should start the car and drive home?"

I—I don't know if I can.

"Sure you can. I promise I'll keep My mouth shut. I don't want you wrecking your car."

Andy started the car and managed to drive home. The voice never spoke, but his ears were dreadfully alert all the way.

He tried to amp down the terror. The voice didn't come into his ears, but his heart did; he felt it pumping, like the steady thump-thump-thump of some artillery.

He scrambled into his apartment, dropped the groceries on the floor and collapsed on the couch. His heart stopped throbbing in his ears. He took slow breaths and stared at the ceiling in the apartment, a plastered landscape. He listened to the silence. Dew-drops bloomed on his face. No melting curtains, all ten fingers intact. I'm not insane, Thank God.

"You're welcome."

The voice shot terror into him. His heart throbbed back in his ears.

"Get out of my head!" he shrieked out.

"Andy, don't scream like that. Settle down, you're not crazy, I promise you. And I will get out of your head—after you do the favor I have to ask of you. "

You don't talk like God.

"How do you know? Have you ever once talked to Me? What do you want Me to do, start throwing a bunch of thees and thous at you? I'm not the threatening kind, Andy. But you owe Me a favor. And it would be better to pay it than not."

"Oh, Please!" Andy crawled off the couch and got to his knees. He clasped his hands in supplication. "Please, just leave me alone!"

"Get off the floor, Andrew. Get off your damn knees. And stop folding your hands in front of you, it creeps Me out. I've had a stomach full of people whimpering on their knees, believe you Me. I never made people to be on their knees, they somehow learned it on their own."

Andy stared up at the bumpled-white ceiling. What's the favor you ask of me?

"It's a small thing," the voice said. "I want you to rescue My daughter."

Andy stared at the ceiling. Then he scrambled off the couch and staggered into the kitchen.

"Andy?"

I need a drink. Maybe four or five. Oh, God! He touched his chest, heard his heart pumping too hard.

"Yes?"

Drink until I pass out and this goes away.

He fumbled the bottle of Canadian whiskey out of the cupboard. Drink yourself to sleep, and this will go away.

"Are you talking to yourself, or Me?"

What? Rescue your...

"My daughter."

The daughter of God.

"Right. Her name is Jessica. She's living in a brutal place right here in Lincoln. A crackhouse. She's only five. I'm asking you to rescue her, to take her out of that place, escape with her to Las Cruces, New Mexico (it's a beautiful place), and raise her there as your daughter. That's not too much to ask, is it?"

Andy ripped the top off the plastic whiskey bottle. He poured with shaking hands. Drink, drink, drink, his mind said. Tomorrow the voice will be gone.

"Not likely, Andy. I won't be gone until you rescue My daughter."

What? Go to a crackhouse and kidnap a five year old girl—are you crazy?

"That's been debated. "

This isn't real anyway, Andy thought. I'm developing schizophrenia.

"No, you're not. Calm down. You go rescue Jessica, get her out of there, and I'll leave you alone. Otherwise…well, I'm kind, but I'm not Santa Claus."

This is what schizophrenia is. Please let this madness leave my mind, God, and I promise: I will never, never ever take acid again. Never again!

"Good. I'm glad to hear that. Now the situation is this, Andy: the crackhouse is located at 526 Dudley Street. That's in the north 27th Street neighborhood."

Andy stared at the plastered ceiling.

"526 Dudley Street," the voice went on. "A crackhouse, an awful place. Skeletons of people lying against the rotting walls, passing a crack pipe. While My sunlight makes such colors and My world is calling out her magic voice. Sorry to be melodramatic, but it's a hell of a waste."

If I go there—if I drive to that address and go up and knock on the door and all that—you'll leave me alone?

"I wouldn't knock on the door. There are paranoid crack fiends in there. A knock on the door would freak them out. And it's going to be at night. Tonight, to be specific, so I wouldn't drink anymore if I were you."

If you were me.

Andy stared at the ceiling, the white landscape of some distant dead planet. I see. All right. If you're God, why can't you rescue her yourself?

"I don't think that's any of your business. My advice is that you slip quietly into the house, and when the skeletons jump up at you, show them cash money right away. There is no electricity in the place, so take a good flashlight. Show them money and quickly tell them that you want some crack and you'll get it and be gone—or something like that."

Andrew stared up at the ceiling. He thought of Rhonda, what she would think of him when he was in the state mental hospital.

"Forget Rhonda," the voice said. "We've got this mission to accomplish."

We?

"Yes. You don't think I'd let you go it alone."

This can't be real.

"Well, slap yourself or something. 526 Dudley Street. Go there and rescue My Jessica. She's brown. She's very skinny and some cruel people call her a little filthy Negro girl. She has dirty pigtails and she's wearing a soiled, smelly dress, and she is filthy at the moment. She has brown eyes. She sits with her doll and sees unending horror day after day."

Andy swallowed hard. His eyes couldn't stay away from the ceiling. You'll be there to protect me?

"Maybe."

Maybe? You're God.

"Thanks for reminding Me. I'll be there. I might not be able to protect you."

What? Listen, if you are God, and this is true, and you can't protect me, there's no way in hell I'm going to walk into a crackhouse and get my ass blown to Kansas.

"Then I guess you'll just have to put up with my nagging for awhile longer. Like forever."

You're not God. If you were, you'd rescue...

"Jessica."

Jessica yourself.

"Andrew, did I ever call on you to show some guts?"

What?

"Guts, Andrew. Did I ever, in the course of your sniveling, worried existence, call upon you to show courage?"

No. I don't suppose...

"Well I am now."

Andy tried to shake away the terror. I can't do this. Not for some voice in my head. Not for some bad acid Stratton pushed on me.

"I'll be with you."

You can't even rescue your own—Okay, this is a flashback, go with the flow. I am not talking to God!

"Why?" the voice asked.

"Be quiet!" Andy yelled out. He stared around his apartment. He took a long drink of whiskey, then another, then another.

"You just have to trust Me, Andy."

No. Trust a crazy voice in my head? Trust an acid flashback?

"My daughter is suffering. I want you to save her."

Kidnap a little girl—then what?

"Then, as I said, you'll have to go into hiding. Las Cruces, I recommend. But Denver's nice, too."

No, I'm not going to do this. It's insane, and I'm not going to do it.

"I'll be with you."

I'm not going to kidnap a little girl and wind up in prison or some psych ward.

"If you don't rescue her, she'll die. And you'll never hear the last of it from Me."

Okay, if you're God—if you're God—why me?

"Why not?"

Grab a little girl out of some drug nest? Kidnap her and go into hiding from the Law?

"It's not as bad as it looks, Andy. Her own mother doesn't care about her. Her mother will be glad to get rid of her. Her only regret will be that she couldn't have sold Jessica for crack."

You're not God! God doesn't talk like you. If your daughter Jessica is suffering and about to die, then You should save her.

"Andy, shut the hell up and listen. You are to drive your Civic to the house at 526 Dudley Street. Whether you believe this is real or not is beside the point. You will be driving up to a crackhouse, and you will have 20 dollar bills in your fist. You'll have to stop at the ATM on your way over there. Once there your only goal is to gather up My little girl and get her out of there. I'll cover you."

Cover me?

"A puff of smoke or a lightning bolt or something. A distraction."

If you're God, you should be able to do better than that.

"Andrew, for once in your life quit being a puss. Do you think I created you and this world so that you could hide out and cower in the shadows of life? Well, I'm sorry, but that's not going to happen. I have mice to do that. I don't want you to be comfortable and safe."

Why?

"Because that's what you've always been, and I'm sick of it."

I don't deserve this. Not for one hit of Orange Sunshine.

"Shut up and listen: whether you believe it or not, when you get to 526 Dudley, there will be a dark, seemingly abandoned crackhouse there. Crack skeletons will likely confront you, and then you wave the money at them. You want to buy dope, that's all. Then you somehow work your way to a room down the hall. Inside is Jessica. You gather her up and get out of there as best you can."

As best I can.

"I'll back you up."

If I drive to that address—if I go up and check the place out and it's not what you say it is—

"Then I'll get out of your mind forever."

Okay.

This couldn't— of course— be real. The address on Dudley Street would turn out to be an ordinary family watching t.v., and then Andy could retreat and let them call him a crazy man, suffering an LSD flashback, but not dangerous.

It was over-stress, that's what it was: the trauma of Rhonda marching out as she had, and the ill-considered dropping of Stratton's poison Orange Sunshine. No more drugs, never ever again. This is a lesson, God, that I will never forget.

"Good."

He drove up to 526 Dudley Street. Twelve-thirty at night. It was a dark, dead house. He swallowed at his throat. You don't go up to a house at this hour without knocking.

"No, don't knock," God said. "The door's not locked; crackheads wander in there at all hours."

Andy got out of his car and walked up to the dark house. What are you teaching me, God?

"I'm trying to teach you to have balls. Now get your head in the game. Here is where you see that this is no acid trip. It's the real thing, Andy."

He walked up the steps and onto the porch. His right hand carried a long and powerful flashlight (the God-voice advised him to have some kind of weapon), and his left hand clutched a wad of twenty dollar bills that added up to a full thousand dollars. This was not truly happening, of course. This was madness.

Never will I drop acid again, he thought.

"Keep your damn head in the game."

He tried the door, and it squealed open on rotten hinges. He played the flashlight inside. He heard the scuttle of things scrambling up, and he shined the flashlight at the money in his hand.

"I just want crack," he whispered. "Then I'll be out of here. I just want to score some dope, that's all."

Skeletons gathered in his flashlight, a disturbed clattering coven.

"Who the fuck you?" one of them asked. The Alpha-skeleton.

"I just want to score some dope," Andy said. "That's all."

"I don't know you. How much money you got?"

"Enough." Andy shined his flashlight down the ugly black hallway. He suddenly panicked and just wanted this over with. "No, forget the dope. There's a little girl back there."

"How you know that?" He saw the Alpha-skeleton pull out a knife. "Who the hell you?"

"I'll pay for her. Then I'll be gone."

"What?"

"I'll buy the girl. Then I'll be gone. You don't have to sell me any dope."

The skeleton stared at him. A white hell-face. "How much you willing to pay?"

"A thousand dollars."

The skeleton studied him in the strange beam of the flashlight. An ugly, blinking thing, its mouth starting ooze. "You got a thousand cash on you?"

Now I'm dead. Oh, God, cut me a break, Andy thought. How can I be in this place? I never believed—now I believe. Okay? I Believe!

"He's stoned, Andy," the voice said. "Back him down. Tell him you've got a gun or something. Do something, Andy!"

"Sell me the little girl," Andy said. "Or I'll kill you." He shined the flashlight into the face of the Alpha skeleton. The man's eyes blinked and shivered at the light.

"I have a semi-automatic pistol under my coat," Andy said. He snapped his thumbnail. "Now the safety's off, and I will either trade a thousand dollars cash for that little girl back there, or I will kill you."

"A child-molester." The skeleton stared at him for a moment. Bony things ratttled in the shadows of this dark rotted house, what must have one day been a living room. This is Hell, Andy thought. Am I going to die in Hell, God? Why can't you talk to me now? Talk to me! Tell me what to do.

"Don't you want that squalling brat out of your life?" Andy said. "For a grand?"

"Okay, she's yours for a grand. Go get her."

Andy flashed the light into the crackhead's eyes. He saw fear there. "Let me take her and you'll have a thousand dollars." He stuck out his coat pocket. "Try and stop me, and you'll die."

"I ain't going to stop you. Not if I get that grand."

"You'll get it when I'm out the door with the girl"

Andy rushed down the hallway, shining the flashlight, expecting to be shot in the back. He pushed open the door and there she was, cowering down, holding onto her doll, a little brown girl in Hell.

"Hello, Jessica," he said. "I've come to take you away from this."

Her brown eyes widened. "You know my name?"

"Never mind. I need to take you out of here. I need to rescue you. Do you understand?"

"Yes." The little girl stood and took his hand. Andy, shining the flashlight ahead, prepared to die.

You're not protecting me, are you, God? he thought.

"I wish I could. But I'm as worried as you are. You never know about evil."

He led the little girl down the hall. Crackheads had come out of their daze and were gathering—no longer like skeletons— but vampires smelling blood. Andy pushed passed them, his flashlight whooshing like a light saber.

"They're too pathetic and weak to stop you, Andy," God said. "I'm actually getting proud of you."

Thanks.

When he got to the door he tossed the thousand dollars onto the stained floor and saw the skeletons dive on the money. He rushed the little girl out into the night and they drove off in his Honda Civic.

"See, that wasn't so bad, was it?" the voice asked.

Now what?

"Now you have a beautiful daughter. Now you take her somewhere and raise her. She'll do well in New Mexico. I gave that state quite a bit of sunshine."

Okay, I did what I was told. But if you're really God, and this is Your daughter, why?

"You ask too damn many questions, Andy. Thank Me for what you have—and thank Me for what you don't have."

I kept My promise—I always do. I never talked to Andrew Keith after that. He took Jessica to New Mexico, he raised her and loved her with all his heart, and saw her become a celebrated professor of Philosophy at the University of Nebraska. Andy didn't do any drugs after that, unless he snuck them behind My back, and I don't think he did.

Was she My daughter? No, I was just screwing around with him. But sometimes when Andy looks out at the stars, I like to tickle him with the thought that—oh, never mind. Folks want to know what God truly loves. It's a good story.

NIGHT OF FROZEN FOG. . .

THE PASSENGERS OF GREYHOUND 176—Denver to Lincoln, Nebraska—stared out at the snow-covered land beyond the bus windows: a ghost prairie.

The sun made no colors as it set behind the silken white distance; the world only felt more gloomy. And ahead down the interstate the fog grew denser.

"Jesus, what a place," Greg Parsons of Florida (Gainesville Electronics), remarked. He wished that he did not have a fear of flying. He would have landed at Eppley field in Omaha by now, on the company's money; and he would be in a safe, warm motel room. Instead, he stared out the interstate at a lost and desolate world, trees like statues of marzipan rising out of hills of sugar. Glimpses of frosted barbwire beyond the veil of winter fog—nothing more. "People do live here," he remarked nervously. "This part of Nebraska, this—place."

"Not many do," said Butch Kane, across the aisle and two seats forward. The old man yawned and stretched. "And I know 'em all. Next stop is where I live, the town of Rose, Nebraska. 170 people."

The other six passengers came alive and stared at the old man. Little five year old Audrey, three rows back, climbed the seat in front of her in order to stare.

The old man had only boarded in North Platte, and he had snored the whole ride since.

"That's a short bus ride," Miss Segal remarked.

Her daughter Audrey peeped over the back of the seat in order to get a glimpse of the old man they had named 'the sleeper'.

"Hi!" she said. "You woke up!"

"Audrey, don't be rude," Miss Segal said. "Get down, don't stare."

"I time my naps pretty good anymore, Darling." Butch Kane winked at the little girl, and she bobbed down below the bus seat.

"You're lucky you didn't try and drive in this." Parson stared out at the fog.

"Well, I got diabetes and it lost me one of my eyes." Butch Kane hooked his arm over the bus seat in order to explain to his fellow passengers: "My heart's one shot gone, you see. I shouldn't be alive, let alone driving, not in this weather. Too many hard spirits and too much tobacco for too many years."

He frowned apologetically at the little girl, Audrey, who was again peering at him.

"Anyway, I don't miss driving. My God, look at that fog."

Mrs. Cage, two seats behind Parson, a woman of fifty with an attractive but terrified face; a woman clutching a leather bag to her stomach, spoke up in a sharply-worried voice: "Is this normal in these parts? This kind of winter fog?"

"Not really," Butch Kane said. "But out here in Nebraska there's no such thing as normal weather."

They were all quiet for a moment; only the grumble of engine and hiss of the bus-wheels, a leather seat groaning, aluminum rails clicking like teeth. How this winter fog took the world into its silence.

Parson stared ahead down the interstate at the blinding white. How can you drive in that?

He glanced at Butch Kane. "Is it going to get worse?"

The old man gave him a blinking frown. He twitched his head toward the seat where the young woman and her little girl were sitting and staring, as all were, at the world outside the bus that was disappearing into a cold white cloud.

"It's only a winter fog," the old man said.

Mrs. Cage fastened on her reading glasses and her chewed fingernails pecked like a frantic chickenhead at her cell phone. Finally she announced, "The temperature here is 38 degrees. It's not that cold out there."

"Thirty-eight degrees isn't cold?" Parson questioned.

"Not if there's no wind," Butch Kane said. "And there's not a breath of wind out there."

Miss Segal shuddered, wrapped an arm around Audrey. "Why don't you try and get some sleep, Baby."

"It's too strange out, Mommy." The little girl stared at the fog. "Like there's no world out there."

Miss Segal shuddered again. "Sir?" she called ahead to the old man.

Butch Kane looked around.

"How long do these winter fogs last?"

"Probably all night and into the morning; until the sun burns some of it away." He addressed all of his fellow passengers, but he hoped particularly that the young driver was listening: "Chances are, folks, the driver'll have to pull over and we'll have to wait it out. Don't worry, he knows what he's doing."

The bus driver was listening, and terrified of what he was doing. Earl Harper, only 22, was beginning to get really scared. He tried to keep his eyes on the pavement, the lane, the dashes on the left and the stripe on the right, and any sign of what might be up ahead, swirling in the bus lights. He had only been driving the bus a little over 4 months. Ordinarily Denver to Lincoln was the most boring stretch ever. Even after such a plains blizzard and so much snow the interstate, once cleared, was a cinch. But he hadn't expected this fog. He blinked his eyes at it; he refused to go over 50.

His eyes darted up and blinked at the interstate, at the white blindness ahead. It was going to get a lot worse.

His mind calculated: next exit was Rose. A gas station there, but no motel. He would fill up the bus, and they would have to wait for that fog to clear. Three miles, could he make it that far?

"When we pull off at Rose and let Mr. Kane out," he announced to his passengers (he tried to sound confident), "I'm going to fill up the bus. But then we're going to have to sit tight and wait for this fog to lift. I'm sorry, I apologize; but it's getting too thick."

"What motels are there?" Parson asked.

"No motels," Butch Kane said. "Just a gas station."

"So we'll have to camp out in the bus?" Miss Segal asked. "Or that gas station?"

"For how long?" Mrs. Cage said, staring into the fog.

"I can't say, Ma'am."

"All right, camping out!" Audrey clapped her hands. "Mommy," she whispered. "Just don't leave me alone with the dark guy."

She looked back at the young man who lay sprawled out over the very last row of bus seats, his knife-shaped cowboy boots crossed over the aluminum and leather in front of him. The guy with long oil-black hair and a savage black beard. The guy who blinked like a snake.

He gave the little girl a slow smile, and Audrey looked away. The young, devil-looking man had boarded at Denver, and had not said a pocketful of words in more than 300 miles of frozen interstate.

He had carried onto the bus only a shabby knapsack and a guitar. From then on, he seemed to dwell in a dark patient silence. He seemed amused, not alarmed at the winter fog out there that was smothering the world.

"Don't worry, Honey." Miss Segal glanced back at the wraith, and he gave her an eerie half-grin, his eyes peering into hers, as if to harvest and eat her fear.

Loose and relaxed he seemed, but his eyes were evil. Miss Segal shivered and looked away.

Parson glanced at Miss Segal, then back at the goth-guy, sprawled like a big black spider over the bus seats in his vicinity. Some over-the-edge musician going for an early over-dose. Even his pants were black, as if that were the only color.

"What do you think of this fog?" he asked.

"It's white." The young man smiled as if he were reading Parson's mind.

"I'm Greg Parson. I'm from Florida."

The spider nodded, still wearing that gentle smile.

Audrey was staring back in nervous fascination. Mr. Parson's calmness made her bold enough to say to the 'Dark Guy': "My name's Audrey. What's yours?"

"Aristotle."

"Aris—" Parson frowned and traded looks with Butch Kane.

"That's a good name," Audrey said. "My last name's Miller, what's yours?"

"Audrey!" her mother hissed. "Get down from there. You don't give out your last name to strangers!"

"Socrates," the young man's voice echoed in the bus. "My name is Aristotle Socrates."

"He has a funny name, Mommy," Audrey whispered.

"Okay, okay!" Earl Harper called back at his passengers: "The exit to Rose is just up ahead. We'll get there, I'll gas up; then we'll just have to wait it out."

"Wait it out." Mrs. Cage gave a wooden face to the world.

Only pray God you can get them there, Earl Harper thought.

His fists gripped the steering wheel, the bus, as if the harder they gripped, the more in control he would be. He stared awestruck into the white world. He glanced at his speedometer. One point seven miles to the Rose Exit; then will I be able to see it?

He slowed the bus down to 35, then twenty-five. He stared into the sudden impossible whiteness, the highway stripes vanishing.

He slowed the bus down to ten miles an hour, praying that some semi or four-wheel drive didn't smash into him from behind.

Driving Blind. The rule is, pull over and stop.

He pulled over, and at that moment he spotted curving dash-marks leading up to a faint halo of light. The exit.

Earl gunned the bus up around a curve and there was Kelsey's Filling Station. Squinting into the neon mist, he manuevered the bus around to get fueled. He stared into the cloudworld. He breathed Thank God relief. He had never been in fog like this, not like this. Even in the blurred lights of the filling station he had to grope the bus to the fuel pump. Finally it sighed to a stop. The bus had made it to the Rose exit.

He gassed open the doors. Fog flowed into the bus. He jumped out and hooked up to the pump. He frowned. The gas pump wasn't working. He stared into the cold fog at the dead glow of Kelsey's Filling Station.

Closed?

"I hope they have beef jerky here," Audrey said, dancing out of the bus on her mother's hand. "Mommy look at it, we're in a cloud!"

"It's—I can't see anything. Here, hold my hand. There's the entrance up there. God, I need coffee."

"This is remarkable," Butch Kane said, climbing carefully out of the bus. "I've seen spring fogs, but not like this. A winter fog like this?"

Parson lept out of the bus, then escorted Mrs. Cage into the fearful cloud-world.

"Thank you, Mr. Parson," she said. She tore her hand from his and began stepping, like a blind woman, through the fog toward the lights of the gas station. A woman clearly on the edge of a breakdown, he thought.

"How far from here do you live, Mr. Kane?" Parson said through the fog.

"Two miles north, up a gravel road somewhere out there."

"You're not going to try and make it home, are you?"

"In this? No, I'd wind up someplace in Kansas. What we all got to do is get some food, snacks and water, then just camp this out in the bus. That's what I plan to do, anyway, as soon as I get a chocolate milk and a bag of peanuts."

The old man vanished in the fog, and Parson groped after him, toward the faraway lights of the gas station. "We have fogs in Florida, of course," Parson called out. "But they're warm."

"This is a strange one," Butch Kane's voice said from the cloud. "This one is really strange."

The lights of the gas station grew brighter, but Parson tripped getting toward the entrance. He looked behind him. Would they be able to find their way back to the bus?

No matter. A trip to the bathroom, an armful of snack food and soda, everything needed to wait out a fog.

But the driver, Earl Harper, gestured them all back. "It's closed," he said.

"It's closed?" Mrs. Cage asked. She stared into the half-dead filling station as if it had betrayed the world.

Butch Kane was staring at the fog. "I don't know if I can believe this," he whispered.

"What do you mean?"

"It's getting worse."

"What?" cried Mrs. Cage.

"The fog."

They all stared into a whiteness, a blindness.

"Okay, Folks," Earl Harper's voice took over, shaking bravely: "We should all get back to the bus and wait this out."

"He's right," Parson said. "Come on, let's go!"

"Everybody grab a hand!" Butch Kane cried.

They managed to daisy-chain their way to the faint yellow light of the Greyhound bus. They all climbed in, Audrey whispering to her mother: "The 'Dark Guy' didn't get off."

"I see that," Miss Segal said. "Here, Audrey, let's get into our seats and wait this thing out."

They tumbled into the bus and made individual nests and stared out at the whiteness. The bus hummed in neutral, and it was warm enough, and the interior lights made yellow shadows.

"My God, look out there!" Parson said. "What is this, Mr. Kane?"

"It's nothing I ever saw before." Butch Kane stared out the bus window at—nothing.

"I can't look at it!" Mrs. Cage cried out, scaring them half to death. "I can't look at it!"

"Calm down," Parson said. "Please, Mrs. Cage. Calm down and have patience."

"It's only a winter fog," Butch Kane said, looking out at it.

"Everybody's getting scared," Audrey said. "Why is everybody getting scared, Mommy?"

"No. Here, lay down and bundle up and go to sleep, Audrey. We're in a bus and we're caught in a fog, and when the fog is over, we'll go there."

"Where?"

"Go to sleep, my daughter," she said.

All of the passengers of Greyhound 176 were curled into their seats now, waiting for the winter fog to lift, to give them some light or form or signal to say that the world was out there. Earl Harper couldn't stare into that white darkness; he studied the mindless glowing lights on the bus's console panel. His only job was to get this bus and these passengers to Lincoln, Nebraska.

Safely. And that means not in this.

Everyone got settled, and coats rustled round. Outside the bus the world vanished in white blindness. No stars or sky or features, no world. You couldn't walk a foot out there.

"I'll keep the bus running," Earl Harper said back. "And we just have to wait this out."

"This is Hell," Mrs. Cage said. "We are all in Hell."

"Mrs. Cage," Parson said. "Don't say things like that."

"Mommy!" Audrey whispered. "That woman just said that we're in Hell."

"No, you don't listen to her."

"It's just a fog," Butch Kane said. "Calm down, calm down."

"Maybe not," a voice spoke out.

They all glanced round at Aristotle Socrates, laying out over the far back bus seats, a spider in white webs of the fog. "Maybe not," he repeated.

"What do you mean?" Parson asked.

"Maybe this is going on everywhere."

"What do you mean, everywhere?" said Parson.

"This blindness. This white fog."

"I'm scared, Mommy," said Audrey.

"Okay, Baby. It's okay."

"It's fog," Butch Kane said back at the young punk. "That's all."

"Maybe it's not."

"What the hell else is it then?"

"I guarantee you it's clear as a bell in Gainesville Florida." Parson glanced back at the goth-guy. The lights in the bus were barely yellow, he saw the guy as a disjointed shadow.

"Who knows?" Aristotle Socrates said. "The end of the world?"

"No, don't say that."

"What's he saying, Mommy?" Audrey asked.

"Nothing. He's trying to scare everybody; he's trying to be mean, that's all."

"Why?"

"I don't know."

"There is something wrong out there," Mrs. Cage said. "Something is wrong with the world."

"It's just a winter fog."

"No, it's not. Things are disappearing!"

"Calm down, Ma'am," Parson said. "We're all caught in a fog—an act of nature—that's all. We just need to wait until it goes away."

"What if it doesn't?" Aristotle Socrates called from his domain at the back of the bus.

"Look, you!" Parson shot out his index finger. "Stop trying to make everyone afraid."

"Now now, we just wait til it's over," Butch Kane said. "That's all we have to do."

The young guitar-man was only a darkish form back there. A shadow under the faint yellow glow of the bus lights, a form the heavy fog was making less distinct.

"I don't have to try to make you afraid," he said.

"It's getting worse."

"I know. Don't worry,' Miss Segal said.

"What if it doesn't go away, Mommy?" Audrey asked.

"What?"

"What if that fog doesn't go away?"

"Oh, Honey, close your eyes and go to sleep. It'll go away. Are you warm enough?"

"Yes." Audrey burrowed up against her tired mother. The bus was all quiet.

Audrey blinked her brown eyes at the fog. Then blinked them away.

"Everybody warm enough?" Earl Harper called softly back.

"I think we're all fine," Parson said. He stared behind him into the dark mists at the statue of Mrs. Cage "Let's just try and get some sleep."

Some of them closed their eyes and tried to sleep. But every sound their eyes would dart like deer into the frozen fog that ruled the world beyond the bus. Fog that was impenetrable.

Audrey squirmed and hoped she wouldn't have to go pee. Everybody was scared. She had been able to hear it in their voices. And now they were really scared, because they were pretending so hard not to be.

Except Mrs Cage: "Sir? Mr. Kane?" she called out of the white world. Her voice was squawky. "Mr. Kane?"

"Yes, Ma'am."

"This fog. We'll have to wait until dawn?"

"Or a little longer," Butch Kane said. "Welcome to Nebraska."

"I can barely see you." Mrs. Cage let out a gasp. "You're all disappearing!"

"We have to keep the windows open a little, Mrs. Cage," Parson's voice said. "It's a regulation to prevent carbon monoxide poisoning."

"We let it in then," she said. "Oh, God!"

"Mrs. Cage…what?"

"We let in the fog!"

"What?"

"She said that we let in the fog," Aristotle Socrate's voice echoed from back there in the shadows. Parson shuddered.

"Fog won't hurt you," Butch Kane's voice said out of the gathered cloud.

"We're not disappearing, are we?" Audrey whispered to her mother.

"Of course not. Now, close your eyes, Audrey."

"We let in the fog!" Mrs. Cage's voice shrieked out.

"No—quiet now," Butch Kane's voice said. "Sit and wait it out, that's all. Try and get some sleep."

Earl Harper, curled up in the driver seat, was listening. "Everybody warm enough?" he called back.

"We're fine!" the dark man's voice echoed from the back of the bus, scaring everybody.

Parson glanced back, but there was nothing. The fog had penetrated the bus, and there was only a yellowy remembrance of the bus lights. He felt his equilibrium give way, a plummeting panic. He closed his eyes and took deep, vaporous breaths.

"Mommy, I can't see anybody," Audrey's voice said.

"Feel my hand, Honey," Miss Segal said.

"I can't see anything!" Mrs. Cage's voice screamed out of the whiteness.

"Now, please don't panic!" Earl Harper cried back. "We're still running, the bus is still running, we're warm enough…"

"I can't see anything!"

"My God!"

"Holy God!"

"This is Hell," said Mrs. Cage. Her voice crunched like a frozen sheet. "I knew I couldn't escape it, not by trying to run."

"I'm scared, Mommy," Audrey whispered. "I'm really scared."

"No, Baby."

Butch Kane had over-heard: "There's nothing to be scared of, Honey. All you have to do is close your eyes."

"But when I close my eyes it's worse," Audrey said.

"Now, get some sleep, Angel." Miss Segal wrapped her daughter into her lap.

"Don't be afraid, Audrey, I'm right over here," Parson said, staring into the dense fog. Those voices out there, other humans caught in this, whatever it was. More than a fog; a vanishing of the world. A world of blindness, a world of silence and mist.

The passengers sat quietly for some time, pretending sleep. The fog surrounded them. They only knew another still existed by the sound of scared breathing.

"Oh God Oh God Oh God!" Mrs. Cage finally cried out.

"Be quiet, Woman!" Butch Kane's voice bellowed. "Try and get some sleep."

"Nobody's going to sleep tonight," the voice of the guitar dark guy came out of the fog. Aristotle Socrates: "We're all blind. I had a good friend, great bass player, he was blind. He told me once that it's hard to get to sleep when you're blind."

"What's that supposed to mean?" Parson said.

"Nothing."

"I think you're laughing. What's so funny about this?"

"We're no longer people," Aristotle Socrate's voice came out of the nothingness. "Now we're only voices. We're not people now, we're sound waves."

"Mommy, what's he saying?" Audrey asked.

"Nothing. Now try and go to sleep."

"Please, folks!" Earl Harper's voice called back. "This is a bad fog. Let's just please wait it out. It's now two thirty in the morning. The sun will rise in a few hours, then visibility will enable me to—"

"Oh God!" Mrs. Cage's voice cried out. "This is how the world ends! This is how it ends!"

"Mrs. Cage, close your eyes," Parson said. "Sit back, try and relax, just go to sleep."

"That's right," Butch Kane's voice said. "You have to wait things like this out."

"We're blind," Aristotle Socrate's voice echoed out. "We're all blind."

"God has made us blind!" Mrs. Cage's voice cried out.

"It's fog, that's all it is, it's just fog," Parson said, holding Miss Segal and her daughter Audrey in his arms.

"I'm sorry to come to you, Mr. Parson." The woman shivered against him. "I'm scared."

"Yes."

"I'm scared," Audrey said out of the fog.

"Yes, I know."

"I can't see your face," Audrey said.

"I can just see yours."

"Everything is scary," Audrey said.

"Well, then it's good we don't get scared," Parson said.

"I can't see you!"

"I know, Audrey. But listen to me, my voice. This is just a winter fog. It's scary, I know, but it will pass. And years from now you'll tell the story of it and you won't feel scared, you'll feel thrilled—and nobody will believe you."

"I can't see anything!"

"Close your eyes, Audrey," Parson said. "You'll see everything if you close your eyes."

"Everybody just needs to calm down," Butch Kane's voice muttered.

Then suddenly Mrs. Cage's shrill voice pierced the fog: "My cell phone's not working! I can't get a signal on my cell phone!"

"Jesus, lady, stop scaring us to death," Butch Kane's voice. "My heart can't take your voice."

"What good is a cell phone anyway," Parson said.

"I wanted information," Mrs. Cage's voice cried out. "How long this fog is supposed to last."

Aristotle Socrates heard the raw terror in her voice—but something else. Shame. Mrs. Cage, ashamed that all the terrors of her life were roosting suddenly in her brain, that she was showing her fear of life so nakedly.

"It's a beautiful fog," his voice echoed out of the cloud. "Why can't we just enjoy it?"

Somehow the voice calmed everyone.

Butch Kane even chuckled. "Are you good on that guitar?"

"Better than most," the dark guy's voice echoed back.

Parson held the young woman and her daughter in the white cloud. "Sleep now," he whispered to them. "Sleep."

"Everybody warm enough?" Earl Harper called back, his voice tripping on fear.

"We're okay," Butch Kane's voice.

The strange fog was everywhere; it had penetrated the bus. It was a supernatural thing, a white horror. There was nothing out there to the eyes.

"Mr. Kane?" Earl's voice asked.

"Yeah?"

"What is this?"

"I don't know, son."

"Well, you live here, this is your place."

"Yeah, all my life. And since I retired, I've come up here to Kelsey's ten thousand times for breakfast."

"What is this?"

Butch Kane blinked his eyes against the blindness. Then he closed them and settled back in the bus seat. "I don't know," he said.

"This is Hell," Mrs. Cage's voice called out. "This is just Hell."

"It's fog," Butch Kane muttered back, his eyes just finding sleep. "Winter fog. It'll go away."

"What if it doesn't go away?" Aristotle Socrates.

The dark man's voice roused Audrey from sleep. She opened her eyes to the horrible white blindness. She sensed the dark man back there, sprawled out on the bus seats.

She called into the white cloud, "It will go away. This fog will go away."

A silence. Then his voice: "You're awake, Audrey. You need to get some sleep."

"It will go away," Audrey said.

"This will never go away," Mrs. Cage's voice scratched the silence. "This white blindness is here forever. This is Hell."

"It'll burn off in the morning," Butch Kane muttered, trying to get back to sleep.

The white cloud in the bus was silent for a long time. Fear burns energy, and finally spends the last of it, and sleep comes like the white fog. Fear hovered over the bus; Earl Harper felt it pinch him as he twitched at a dream, and called to a high school sweetheart.

Audrey stared back into the cloud. Back where the dark guy was. "Are you going to sleep?" her voice called back. "Everybody else is."

"I don't sleep much," his voice came out of the whiteness.

"I'm falling asleep," Audrey said.

"Good."

Dawn was no more than a pinkish bloom; but as the sun rose, the fog dissipated, cloudy air dissolved, and the Nebraska hills outside the bus showed themselves, white hills of snow, appearing under bluing skies.

Audrey's eyes blinked open. "I can see!" she said. Then she closed her eyes and hugged her mother and tried to go back to sleep.

Passengers stirred, blinked their eyes at the clearing world. Mrs. Cage began softly moaning at God.

Earl Harper roused himself and stared thankfully at the purple sun that swirled in the frozen morning mist. He rubbed his face awake. "Pretty soon," he called back to his passengers, "we'll be able to get back on the interstate to Lincoln."

Butch Kane roused himself and gathered his travelling bag. "Well, so long, folks," he said.

Parson woke up and looked at him. "You're going home?"

Butch Kane grinned at him: Miss Segal and her daughter Audrey were asleep in his arms, a trio making a nest on a bus seat.

"Yeah, I'm going home. My house is only two miles down the road. I'll make it that far now." He looked back into the mists still clinging to the back of the bus: "Keep playing that guitar, young man. You might get famous."

"I will," said the dark guy.

Butch Kane winked at Parson. "I didn't think he was asleep. And I don't think you are either, Miss Audrey."

The little girl blinked guilty brown eyes up at him. "I heard you talking. Bye bye, Mr. Kane."

Butch Kane smiled out the bus window. "See how pretty that purple sun is out there, Audrey?"

"What happened last night scared me," Audrey said. "That Mrs. Cage screaming."

Butch Kane looked back at Mrs. Cage, who sat in exhausted and wooden shame.

"What really scared you, Audrey?" Butch Kane asked.

A voice from the back of the bus. Aristotle Socrates: "Good question."

THE SPREAD...

WHEN I TRIED TO look into Dr. Erickson's eyes I knew the world had ended. I had known it all along, but Hope is a tough and irrational nut.

"The drone's returned." I tried to look into her eyes, but they were on the floor.

"Yes."

"Don't worry," I said. "It might be what I expected, but it can't be worse than that."

"Don't worry?" Now her grey eyes pounced on mine: "Don't worry." She sobbed out a chilling laugh: "It's what you expected. It looks like the moon out there! Nothing but desert and trillions on trillions on trillions of dead nanos. They cover the earth like…"

"There's not much left for them to eat."

"Dr. Porter…" Her whole body trembled and twitched. I loved her; yet I studied her as I've always studied everything. My Super Ego had always had the habit of detaching itself from my Id; all my life I had the ability (or curse), of not really living life, but studying it.

How strange that now, on this doomed island on Earth, I thought about the difference between terror and horror. Terror is sudden—you can't expect it. It jabs your fight-or-run button. Terror is Id, unexpected, quick; the hawk grabs the mouse.

But a journey with horror is a very long and different one. How slow and aching and infinite it can be. Something not here yet, but coming with mathematical certainty. Horror has nothing to do with instinct, and everything to do with conscious mind making slow, smeary photographs of what will come: Horror is slow. Horror is your mind eating itself...

"Anyway," Dr. Erickson collected herself, a scientist once more. "Do you want to see the pictures the drone brought back?"

"No, I don't see the point. If there's not much time left—and there isn't— I don't see why it should be wasted on futility. It's more important that I stay here and monitor the radio. Colonel Stone should be calling in soon with more bad news."

"If the spread can be contained before it reaches our mountain," Dr. Erickson said. "It could die of starvation."

"They don't die. They just shut down."

"Still, when they shut down they die, for all practical purposes."

I stared out of the complex at the world beyond our green island. Dead moonscape, mindless existence: "I wonder if our moon once had intelligent life—if Mars ever did—and if they made their world, as we did, into what it is now."

"You're scaring me, Dr. Porter."

"I'm sorry. I don't mean to."

"If we can find a way to stop this plague..."

"Where have I heard that before? I guess the first time was with Fat John, the great genius. How his jowls drained of color when he was scared. The problem is; it's not a plague. A plague is controlled by nature—or at least limited by her. But this is no product of nature. A plague destroys much of what it touches, but not all. Things created by nature will only destroy so far. Swarms in nature may eat everything green, but not brown. Swarms eat whatever moves, but not what stands still. In the end self-preservation stops them from destroying themselves. These things have only the immediate signal to eat. To eat everything that contains energy. Beyond that, they don't care that they are destroying even themselves—they don't Know they're destroying themselves."

"They're machines. Machines can be stopped."

"That's the problem. They're machines."

The radio beeped, making us both jump. I found Colonel Stone's signal. "This is Base," I said.

Colonel Stone's voice was controlled, but I heard the tension: "Dr. Porter, we presently have the Nanos contained in the valley, but it doesn't look like we'll be able to hold them off for long until we get more spray."

I traded looks with Dr. Erickson. She had the long, tired look of horror on her face.

"There is no spray, Colonel," I said.

The radio was silent for several moments. "We can't stop them without more spray, Dr. Porter."

"We're working on producing more," I lied. "In the meantime, keep pushing back. Hold out as long as you can."

"This thing is becoming impossible to stop," Colonel Stone said.

"Yes, I know. It's constantly adjusting, mutating. Hold out as long as you can, Colonel. Then get your people up the mountain."

I shut off the radio. Then I unplugged it so that no new messages could arrive. I looked at Dr. Erickson. "I'm afraid the colonel is right: these things can't be stopped."

The blood had drained from her face. She was only in her thirties, but she looked like an old woman. "So this is the end."

"Not yet," I said. "But soon."

"Oh God!" She cradled her exhausted head in her hands. "It doesn't make sense! That organisms would destroy everything, knowing they were destroying themselves—it doesn't make sense!"

"I'm afraid it makes perfect sense. If a machine malfunctions and starts a fire, will it put out the fire in order to save itself? No, it will melt in the inferno and then be no more. Fat John once commented to me, over gin and tonics, that the greatest safeguard is the power of self-protection. And that his greatest fear was that the Nanos might become not only instruments of homicide, but suicide as well. How tragic that so many of his theories have come about."

"Fat John," she said. "Destroyer of the world."

"Who would ever have thought?"

Fat John, of all people, managed to destroy Planet Earth.

How ignorant we all were to believe in ourselves, in our power. All things that achieve power and domination believe they are invincible. That is what finally destroys them.

I stared down at the dead radio, knowing Colonel Stone was at this moment frantically trying to contact me; that his men were retreating from the organized swarm of tiny robots that marched against him, devouring all organic energy in their path. It's path, because it wasn't mere individual machines, but an evolving carpet of machines that only sought to eat energy and to grow—nothing else, not even self-preservation. Maybe it was the ultimate instinct, to destroy everything.

"For God's sake, plug the radio in!" Dr. Erickson shrieked out.

"Why?"

"Those men are out there fighting those things, giving us time. We owe them—"

"Those men are dead."

THE MINI-BEE...

"ROFESSOR LEO, THERE ARE two men outside who need to speak to you right away. They're—"

"What!!"

Jack Leo glared up from his microscope and jerked the glasses down from the top of his bald head to his nose. He shot the young technician that Ghengis Khan look: being disturbed always sent the old man into a homicidal rage.

It couldn't be helped. "Sir, they're from National Security. They say right away."

Dr. Leo felt his stomach tighten. He got up stiffly from his lab chair and, as always, rubbed his crabbed hands smartly over his neck and shoulders before moving.

"They want to speak with you outside the building, Sir."

"I see." The words *National Security* poisoned the air. He frowned at the young technician, a computer-boy not six months after his PHD.

"Sorry, Sir. They need to see you immediately."

"Yes, you should be."

Dr. Leo grumped his way to the elevator, his mind worrying over possibilities. Is it ebola—or the long-awaited anthrax?

The NS men, a pair of sober bookends, blue necktie and red, met him at the front entrance and escorted him down the concrete steps and away from the building.

Finally Jack Leo had had enough. "All right!" he snapped. "I'm an old man, I can't walk far. What is this?"

"Dr. Leo," Redtie said. "Our apologies for—"

"Never mind that—what is this?"

"Do you know who Dr. Nels Strohm is?" Redtie asked, getting to the point.

Dr. Leo stared at the question. "Of course. At the moment, the most famous scientist in the world. His team works at the Hadron Collider at CERN. He's been in the news lately." He gave Redtie a puzzled look. "What's he got to do with me?"

"He's here now," Bluetie finally spoke up. "And he needs to see you immediately."

What?

"To see me. He's here at CDC?"

"No, a facility not far from here. Koenig Laboratories."

"He knows I'm a bio-chemist, not a physicist—doesn't he?"

"Yes, Sir. It's urgent that you come with us."

"Now?"

"Yes, Professor."

On the ride to Koenig Labs (Dr. Leo knew the place well; they had been trying to recruit him for decades), his frowning mind tried to puzzle this out. Nels Strohm was currently the most celebrated scientist on earth, his team at CERN having created a miniature black hole that they had made stay open—they claimed—a full 45 seconds.

What the hell does smashing particles together have to do with me? And why not just meet at the CDC? Damn somebody, this was high security.

Security meaning *Secrecy.*

"I wish I had a Rolaids," he muttered. Neither blue nor red tie commented.

Dr. Nels Strohm proved to be amiable enough: A young fellow, late 50's, a bit grey and withered, and with an irritating pair of eyes that seemed always to be staring off.

Dr. Leo offered his congratulations for Strohm's achievement: "It seems you've opened a hole in the universe...all the way, maybe, to the Nobel Prize."

"Thank you," Strohm said. "Dr. Leo, please forgive me for being abrupt. There's something I need to show you."

Half an hour later they were suited up and entering a sealed lab no different than the many at CDC, a sterile capsule of computers and instruments. Behind the array of technology was the Isolation Room, its pane wall penetrated only by two slinky robot arms that could reach inside the protective glass.

Jack Leo's stomach flared up again.

He saw a glass slide inside the Isolation Room, housed in a small Plexiglas cube. A high-power microscope connected to the computer was focused on the slide.

To Dr. Leo, this was all quite familiar. Yet his stomach told him different.

"Look at this on the screen, Jack, if you would."

He studied the computer screen that magnified a brown sphere resembling a tiny rusted ball bearing.

"First," Strohm said, startling him. "I need to quickly explain what we might have here. Have you ever read any of Dr. Max Goldman's black hole theories?"

"His big one; the one in SCIENCE."

"Yes. What can you tell me about his ideas?"

Dr. Leo glared out of his glasses at the younger man. These punk geniuses, always wanting to give tests. Let's see how the doddering old man does:

"If I read them correctly, Nels, they speculated that black holes actually puncture the space-time fabric. Unimaginable gravity and energy warps space-time so intensely that it punctures it, creating a black hole. Like pushing a pin into the membrane of your skin until it punctures it."

"Yes."

"Did I pass the test, Nels?"

"And that beyond the puncture could be another dimension, or universe.'

"It's hardly a new theory."

"What do you think of it, Jack?"

"I'm not a Physicist. But I do suspect that it's largely crap—at best."

Dr. Strohm smiled in spite of himself. "I'm hoping you're right," he said. "Less than a week ago we managed to create the mini-bee and keep it open for around 45 seconds."

"Mini-bee."

"Miniature black hole. Some of the younger members of my team started calling it that."

"I see." Dr. Leo didn't approve of younger team members—nor cute scientific nicknames.

"It closed up again and vanished. But in its place our sensors detected...this." Dr. Strohm indicated the computer screen.

Dr. Leo's face went blank for a moment; then his eyes darted back to the screen, the strange brown pebble. Perfectly spherical and smooth. He read the magnification.

"You must have weak sensors. This thing is as big as a spore."

"Our sensors can detect anything as small as an atom," Strohm said. "Which is about the size this was when it was detected."

Dr. Leo glanced at him. "Are you saying..."

"It's growing; and at an alarming rate."

Jack Leo looked back at the computer screen. "It could se some kind of mold." He frowned, doubting it. "Not one I can identify by sight." He allowed himself a malicious snort. "If it is, then you have a bit of a contaminated lab."

"That's close to impossible," Strohm said. "It should be sterile down to the sub-atomic level."

"Sometimes close and should are all nature needs."

"It worries us that it appeared at the exact location where the mini-bee closed."

Dr. Leo scowled. Why were these Physicists always trying to be so precious with their stupid nicknames? He stared at the tiny brown sphere on the computer screen. "I'll have to do some studies on it to determine if it's some kind of fungus or spore. It doesn't look organic."

"Yet, it's growing. More than growing, it's accelerating."

"It could be some chemical reaction brought on by your experiment."

"We've thought of that." Nels Strohm stared away for a few moments, then seemed to be speaking to himself: "We kept the mini-bee open 45 seconds. There could be a very strange phenomenon involving that. It's a speculation based on Hawking's theory that black holes not only absorb, but emit."

"All right. That's a far cry from punching holes into other dimensions."

"Yet it opens up disturbing possibilities. That black holes aren't the one-way streets we thought they were."

Dr. Leo stared at the man for several seconds. Strohm didn't seem mad, but you never know with Physicists.

"You're not telling me what I hope you're not telling me."

Strohm gave him a worried smile. "Probably not. But we have to consider every possibility. When we began our project at CERN, some scientists actually suggested that opening a mini-bee could cause the entire earth to be sucked into it."

"And the A-bomb was going to ignite the earth's atmosphere. Well, you fellows opened one up and it didn't destroy the planet."

"It's not a matter of whether the lab was contaminated or not; it's that this appeared exactly where the mini-bee closed."

Dr. Leo shrugged. "I'll give this thing a thorough study. But I'm not a fan of the Wizard of Oz—and I'm so old I saw it in the theater."

"Give this every test you can—but here, not at CDC. I don't need to tell you to keep your findings…"

"You don't need to tell me."

"One thing I do want to tell you, Dr. Leo." Strohm stared at the glass barrier, the tiny slide in its crystal box. "No, I don't want to tell you, I want to ask you."

Dr. Leo frowned. "Yes?"

"Please keep in mind this: you said that the formation of a black hole is like pushing a pin into your skin, far enough in so that suddenly it punctures the skin."

"I'm no Physicist. I don't pretend to know the mathematics of the things."

"But please consider this, Jack: when the pin punctures your thumb, what happens next?"

Two weeks later the exhausted skeleton of Dr. Jack Leo sat across a desk from the world's most famous Physicist. They traded worried and bloodshot eyes for several moments. Then finally Strohm spoke: "One hundred percent carbon. That seems impossible. One hundred percent carbon is diamond."

"Not this." Dr. Leo was staring down at the desk. He had never felt so frail and bone-weak in his life. Damn damn damn, was all his brain could summon at the moment. He rubbed absently at his bald head, trying to get the blood back in there. "I never believed it was a living organism…impossible. Until it began sprouting those leaders. It's behaving like a—super virus." He looked down at the desk. "My God, I wish I'd never studied anything in my life."

Both men were silent for many moments. Dr. Strohm had read the instrumental and computer analyses, more than once.

"Where do you think it came from, Jack?"

"I can't say. But my computer projections show it completely smothering planet earth in less than ten years."

"If you applied that growth rate to common moss it would show the same," Strohm said.

"Common moss doesn't have this growth rate."

Both men sighed. Dr. Leo stared down at the desk.

"What do you recommend, Jack?"

"Kill it," Dr. Leo said to the desk. "We need to find a way to kill it as fast as we can."

Dr. Strohm let the silence fall slowly before speaking: "The Surgeon General and the CDC are already making preparations—"

"Kill it, Nels." Dr. Leo traded stares with the Physicist. "You know," he accused. "You know."

Dr. Strohm's eyes grew disturbed. "They want more time to study it."

"Kill it."

"Jack, you of all men should know how important it is to study something like this—while it's alive. Finding its secrets."

"It's not a matter of finding secrets," Dr. Leo said. "It's a matter of finding a way to kill it."

"I don't have that authority."

"For the love of God!" Dr. Leo stared down at the desk.

"Somebody much more powerful than I…well, they've ordered that more tests and studies need to be made until…"

Dr. Leo addressed the desk: "Nels, I've been a bio-chemist for over 50 years. Working at the CDC I've made exponential growth of organisms—diseases, bacteria—my life's work; to try and predict the speed and distances that plagues and diseases might progress across the globe. This—this is off the charts. This growth rate…the composition of the thing…"

Strohm's eyes were blinking like Morse Code. "We either have time, or time has come to an end. Yes, I know, Jack."

"The data only tell us two things," Dr. Leo said. "One is terrifying, the other horrifying. Can we get our knucklehead government to understand?"

"I don't know," Strohm said. "It's growing at a terrifying rate."

"It's terrifying. But not horrifying. What's horrifying?"

"I know, Jack. How can we stop it?"

"I don't think we can."

"Do you think it came out of their mini-bee?" Dr. Andrews asked him.

"The term is Miniature Black Hole." Dr. Leo automatically frowned at his younger colleague. "It doesn't matter where it came from."

The government compound, not long ago the privately owned Koenig Laboratories, was now desperately trying to house a super-carbon being that defied all analyses, all power on earth, and was growing on a schedule that would in six months approach the speed of light.

Dr. Andrews gave Jack a gentle look. "We'll find a way to stop it, Jack."

"How, damn you!" Dr. Leo exploded. "This is a structure not only expanding exponentially, but evolving at the same rate. It's found an environment—here!—where it has no competition, no enemies. You've seen the looks on the faces of the *great* chemists and geologists who've studied the data."

"Disbelief," Andrews said. "Fear."

"Fear, terror then horror. I'm in the horror stage already. This carbon structure—well, no power that we have on earth can stop it. You know this. We can't begin to stop it."

Andrews was only a child of 40, but a brilliant bio-chemist just the same. He'd braved the villain ebola in Africa and was writing a book arguing against the Black Death being bubonic plague, the mysterious stranger that had showed up and nearly wiped Europe off the map.

Now, young Andrews was staring away and shaking his head, completely lost in fear. "I always wondered if it would be religion or science that would destroy the world." Andrews couldn't stop trembling. "I—can't—really believe this, Jack."

Dr. Leo made a lemon frown. I'm not afraid enough? No, not afraid, scared. Afraid is too mild a word.

Scared.

"Do you pray?" Dr. Andrews asked.

"What?"

"Do you ever pray, Jack?"

The old professor was Ghengis Khan again. "Pray?"

"To God."

"That's nobody's business. Our business right now is to try and stop the inevitable by making the impossible."

Andrews was staring away in disbelief, as all the geologists and chemists and physicists had. Andrews wore a disturbing crooked smile. "I pray. I pray that it will go away, back where it came from. I pray that everything could be—"

"Well, it's not," Dr. Leo said. "Good God, here comes my heart attack."

He felt a sudden loss of body control; his mind started to go black and he automatically fingered his heart. Horror made his heart shudder for long vivid moments.

He bent over and took long deep breaths. Seventy-five years old and to see the end of the world...

His mind cleared slowly, as if it were a boat coming out of a fog and there was the shore. Not only the shore. Beyond the fog of consciousness he saw a light. A sudden light peeked into his mind.

"Back where it came from." He looked over at Andrews.

"I may be our only chance," he said to Nels Strohm.

"Take it back to CERN," Strohm agreed. "We have to try."

The super-carbon virus (Dr. Leo couldn't help but think of it that way), was sealed in a steel and aluminum casing that resembled a zeppelin. Then lifted by four navy helicopters away from the unfortunate grounds of Koenig Labs.

Scientists, including Dr. Leo, had urged speed on the syrup-footed

U.S. government. The container need not be any stronger than necessary to carry the virus back to Switzerland. Make it roomy and light. After all, it didn't matter what the container was made of.

The super-carbon structure was itself still almost weightless at this point. Yet its composition redefined the word *indestructible*. It didn't matter if the container carrying it back to Switzerland was made of the strongest titanium or ten foot thick reinforced concrete walls—or toilet paper. The carbon structure would swat aside anything known to man. Nothing could affect it: oxygen, or lack of—blistering lasers—heat far beyond the sun—massive sprays of every devil from atomic radiation to intense gamma rays—super-acids that could scald and eat solid granite…

At least, Dr. Leo thought with some malice, as he watched the silver container mow the night toward the Atlantic. At least it will be in the hands of the damn Swiss. They never got their hands dirty before.

If this didn't work, then damn-it-to-hell nothing mattered.

Could it have come from another dimension, universe? Dr. Leo remembered the beloved movies of his boyhood, when Flash Gordon would face the horrifying monsters out there. The cheesy black and white vision of outer space, the villains out there that had made him spill his popcorn.

He stared out at the warm Georgia night, starlight restless in the humid atmosphere. His mind couldn't get rid of the calculations, the projections, chemical and structural analyses, and he wondered if finally he was going mad.

More likely, having the long-awaited stroke, or heart attack.

He touched his chest and tried to count the beats. But he gave up. He stared at the dots of light that carried the thing back to Switzerland, to CERN.

How awful it can be to know. Everyone going about merry ways, children playing, couples making love. Gardens growing, the wind blowing, the world in lovely balance. The universe—Oh God, ruptured!

Stop this, you coward! Damn your heart, it'll do as it pleases.

What did Dad say to us kids all those long years ago, as he went to unbuckle his belt: "Nix the sniveling; or the belt's coming off."

This could work, he thought as he stared eastward toward the

Atlantic Ocean. All stranded things have an instinct to want to go home.

A month later Dr. Nels Strohm sat across from him in the CDC cafeteria, the bastard wolfing the T-bone Steak Special. Dr. Leo himself crunched at a salad and fruit dish.

"You're eating healthy, Jack."

"My heart. It's been acting up lately. Thought I'd give it a break." He stared hatefully at Strohm's steak. How could a man who'd managed to threaten the planet with certain death now sit there and enjoy that steak?

"Dr. Leo, you may well have helped to save humanity." Strohm, chewing the steak, gave him a victorious look.

"May have?"

Strohm dipped another bite of the steak into A-one sauce, then gave it to his teeth. Dr. Leo frowned a baby tomato into his mouth. "Tell me how it was."

Strohm now chewed contentedly at his smothered-in-butter-and-sour cream baked potato that fondled the T-bone steak. Dr. Leo's own stomach allowed in, with a shudder, a carrot shard.

"We managed to create an energy level far beyond any ever created by man. I was afraid that the Hadron would suffer a start-up collapse. But she worked like a charm, and she created a mini-bee that stayed open a full 68 seconds."

Dr. Leo burped on a radish. "And nine seconds in the thing vanished."

"Nine seconds in the entire structure blinked away."

"Blinked away."

"Now we know where this organism came from." Nels Strohm's eyes were feverish. "We know what it is!"

"No, we don't have the slightest idea what it is—was."

"Was." Strohm stabbed his fork so far into a bite of the steak that it was able to pick up a chunk of the smothered baked potato, all of which he crammed into his Physicist face.

Dr. Leo tried not to despise the man, his steak, his smothery baked potato: "It is was, isn't it?"

"It is was," Strohm said. "It's over."

"For the time being." Dr. Leo glared down at his tasteless salad. "It just vanished. Into your mini—miniature black hole."

"There seems to be a quantum process that's going to need a lot more research to understand."

"A process you fellows monkeyed around with and almost got us all killed."

"Jack—"

"Us all!"

"Discovery is the most dangerous trait of mankind." Dr. Strohm rowed his knife across the just-pink slab of steak in a sweater of crisp gritted char. The baked potato steamed faint butter and sour cream over the table. "Science is a dangerous voyage, Jack."

Jack Leo almost upended the table. No heart on earth was worth this. The bastard!

"I hope you're not all crazy," he said.

"That I hope too."

Dr. Leo's salad smiled up at him, red, orange, purple, green green green. A lovely postcard to his heart that tasted like a postcard.

"How's your steak?" he snarled.

"Very good. Very, very good," Strohm said. "Jack, this is—was—the greatest…this proves so many things! This was the greatest experiment in the history of Science."

"This was letting death out of the box and just managing to get him back in."

"We opened a door to another reality."

Dr. Leo stabbed at a ruffle of lettuce. "Let me tell you a story about reality, Nels: when I was about 12 or so a friend of mine—my best friend—Luther Ruhe, made a gigantic firecracker. He was a brilliant kid, fascinated by chemicals and what they could do. He wanted to explore the secrets of energy, and to unleash them, and to show off for the Morgan girl—Polly I think her name was. Luther would have been a great chemist if he hadn't blown himself to shreds. He made a firecracker so big that he didn't actually understand it, and what it could do. And it blew his head into a basement wall. Why did he do that, Dr. Strohm?"

Strohm chewed thoughtfully at his steak. "He was curious."

"Or stupid," Jack said.

ROSCOE THE BALLOON CLOWN...

I STEPPED INTO THE house, looking over my shoulder at the kids in our backyard wearing sparkly hats, shooting colored tongues out at each other as they honked on their party whistles, holding balloons that bobbed in the wind.

They were all swarming round the table—sprinkled pixies and elves—the table where the clown seemed to have passed out: I looked at Danny; he would have a good 7th birthday. We had paid so much.

"Honey! I think that Balloon Clown—"

"What!" her wild voice shrieked at me from the kitchen; she was trying to attend the birthday cake, a cartoon of chocolate and white ooze.

"Please don't bother me now," she grouched as I entered the kitchen. "Is Danny having a good time?"

"Well..."

She glared around.

"The balloon clown might be drunk." I looked out the window. The children were tying balloons onto the chair where slumped Roscoe, balloons of every color dancing above him.

"I think that clown has passed-out."

"What?"

"Here, look out the window."

"He's not dead, is he? Go out and see!"

"Pray it's not a heart attack."

The children were still tying balloons to the clown's chair as I dashed toward him. A disturbing form: alabaster face, wriggly red hair, handball nose, his costume a Wonder Bread wrapper. I smelled cheap whiskey. Roscoe wasn't dead, damn him; I heard his nose snort and saw spittle leaking out of his mouth.

Good God.

I stood and blinked at the backyard; birthday streamers and balloons. Children running, gathering the colored balloons that dangled everywhere in the yard. Little elves dashing about grabbing the balloons that danced fruit-flavored over their heads.

"No, kids—whoa." I planted myself in front of them. "You shouldn't—you probably shouldn't approach this clown."

"We want to tie more balloons on!" The children cried out at me. "We're finally having fun!"

"I know. But this clown…" I glanced at the kitchen window where my wife stared down like a murderous portrait. "But kids, this—Roscoe the Balloon Clown—well, he's not—"

"Dad, we were finally having fun," Danny said, his eyes pleading. "Come on, Dad! Please!"

I studied the passed-out clown, liquor-spit streaking his white makeup. He was a dead lightbulb. "Okay, tie a few more balloons onto his chair," I said to them.

The kids cheered me, and I winked at Danny's grin. "But I'm going to have to talk to your mother, Danny. Go on, have fun—but she's about to serve the cake."

"Look!" a little girl said. "Every balloon makes him bob up and down more."

"I love you, Dad!" Danny tied his red balloon to the bouquet of bright-colored bubbles that rose above the—sleeping clown.

It's okay, that's his job, I thought. To entertain kids. Roscoe, if you make my son's 7th birthday one to remember, I will not press charges. And I'll keep my wife from pressing them.

I stepped back into the house. "Okay, they're having fun," I said.

My wife marched out of the kitchen. "Fun doing that to an old drunk?"

"He's a professional. It's his job, Honey, to make the kids happy, see they have fun. Look out there! See how much fun they're having? Look at Danny going after those balloons."

My wife looked out the window. She made a face of disbelief: "Oh My God."

"What, Honey!" I ran to the window. "Did he wake up? Is he hurting one of the kids?"

"No, he's—"

I stared out at the backyard, the sparkling birthday party, all for Danny, all so he would take away good memories…

Roscoe the Balloon Clown (still dead in the chair), was floating over the backyard. Worse, he was rising. Or the chair was rising, propelled by the mountain of colored balloons above his snoozing head. I could not believe what I was seeing. The children all stared at the clown in the lawnchair, as he floated away into the night. The upper winds caught him, and he sailed away into the darkness like an odd nightmare.

This didn't happen. Helium? No, this didn't happen. All those balloons tied to the clown's chair…?

"Dad, where did he go?" Danny asked me. "Was it because we tied so many balloons to his chair? Because we knew he was getting lighter, and that made us tie on more balloons?"

I frowned. "No. It was just an accident. You forget this birthday, Danny. Next year will be so much better!"

SAVING SADIE...

IN NEBRASKA THERE ARE January nights that will kill you if you step into them. The wind chill is more than 30 degrees below zero and blowing steadily at 40 miles an hour. The white blizzard roars out of Canada and you are trapped in it, and the furnace won't stop running and you tack blankets and towels over the windows to keep the north away and the snow out of the windows and finally you just sit scared and I sat scared inside my trapped farmhouse and listened to it out there, beyond the windows and beyond the doors and I wondered when the electricity would go out, like God closing his eyes.

And what then, alone in the icy darkness, trying to live through this?

I was smothered in long underwear, sweatpants, two sweaters and a winter coat, a foolish stocking-cap. The television still worked, and I had it tuned to the local station, the grim, suited grey-wrinkled-blinking weatherman who could not emphasize enough the scope and danger of this blizzard. When he said "Absolutely life threatening conditions" I switched the channel to something else, I don't know what. I listened to the awful wind. Two pairs of wool socks. One full glass of bourbon. Cigarettes until they ran out.

The cold was not so terrible; it was the wind. It was the wind that really wanted to kill you. In Nebraska everything is the wind Thermometers understand the cold, but not the wind: out there beyond my scrawny farmhouse was a *Super-phantom*, cold beyond man.

The best description I've ever heard about these winter nights, is *blistering cold.* It was going to be a dreaded white-plains roaring horror, and I curled down into the couch as I did with other storms, and thought about that courageous Nebraska school teacher all those years ago, who led her class through one of these, and got very lucky.

This was not like the spring storms of Nebraska, when God explodes in rain and wind and fast but short violence; when you can creep out afterwards in shorts and tennis shoes to see the strange sun and the destruction. This was long. This was relentless. This was more hateful and would not go away after an hour of violence. It would leave mountains of snow behind it. It would leave deadly cold air behind it for—how long?

Okay, I thought, sipping at the bourbon, hearing that wind and lashing snow. Just crumble down into the couch and wait it out. The cup might be frozen, but it's half-full. The power hasn't gone out yet.

I had the furnace checked less than two years ago, it'll hold up.

Jesus, that wind! Wait it out, wait it out. Just hunker down and survive this.

Then beyond the wind I thought I heard a yelp coming from the neighbor's farm.

Oh, God.

I thought of their dog, a big black Newfoundland named Sadie.

No.

They always kept Sadie in her cramped kennel. Neighbor Tom Klaus had explained to me once that it was because: "She's an outdoor dog".

Whenever I drove past their place, I couldn't help but look over at the dog. Sadie always sat there obediently in her tiny cage of chainlink, her feces unscooped, littering her world. A big ragged scruff of a dog who always looked sad.

They couldn't leave her out in something like this.

She'd freeze to death out in something like this.

Then again I thought I heard that wail…

God, I can't do that, I thought. No—no, oh no. It's death out there. Going a half mile with the blizzard against my back, okay—but back a half mile into the teeth of it? Thirty below zero and that eye-freezing wicked snow?

The Ten-eleven news said not to go out there.

Suddenly the television turned to floating icons as I lost the satellite signal. Now there was only the screaming opera of wind and snow, the screaming snow-wind.

I was still warm in my little farmhouse. But out there past the door was glittery death.

Okay. No can do, I'm sorry.

Then the wind calmed for only a moment, and I heard her yelping, and it was the neighbor's dog. I couldn't give that to the wind.

God damn me, I wrapped myself up as best I could.

I layered myself with another sweatshirt, drew my goose-down winter coat tight about me—wrapped the most important item, my wool scarf round my mouth, and plunged into the blizzard.

If you live in Nebraska, you're a fool if you don't have at least one wool scarf—a long one.

Why am I thinking this?

I stepped into the terrible north wind, my farmhouse door snapping shut like a mousetrap behind me; and I knew beyond the bourbon I had drank, that I was walking at death.

Keep your goddamn mind on that sound!

I heard it again, and I struggled over the snow toward it: a long howl, then a whimpering cry, far off over the hill.

I knew this pasture well enough, but tonight it was a dead planet, savage white. I waded toward the neighbor's property, my coat sizzling in the blizzard. I could see their barbwire fence glittering and twitching in the wind. I managed to crawl over the damn thing, ripping my goose-down coat and leaving some of it in the barbs. I stumbled up to the dog kennel and pulled down my scarf. There was Sadie, stepping her feet desperately at the cold, her coat frozen to her back, her eyes staring at me. I had never seen more intense eyes in my life.

My glove pounded at the frozen kennel latch and got the thing open. "Come on, Sadie, let's go."

She studied me, and cringed back whining into her frozen world.

"Come on, Sadie, follow me! Follow me, Girl!" I ducked down into the chainlink kennel, got behind her and, my boots crunching crystallized turds, pushed Sadie out of the kennel. She walked obediently into the horrible wind, ice stuck to her face. Her coat clattered.

"Come on!" I yelled at her. "Up there, over the hill!"

Sadie shivered in the awful wind. She looked back at the kennel.

"Come on, follow me!" I yelled. Then I turned and went back

against that wind toward my house. The dog could follow me now, or not. God—God—oh, God…

I kept my head down against the wind and the snow. This is 30 below wind, I thought, trudging over the hill. That hateful snow! Jesus, this is bad!

Finally I saw the lights of my farmhouse, and knew that I'd make it.

I took a break, lowered my scarf and looked around at the hills that swept white ghosts across the pasture. My God, that wind! That awful wind.

I glanced down and was surprised to see Sadie trembling at my side. I stared into the blizzard, afraid of this world. "Just down the hill, Sadie!" I yelled at her. "This thing's getting worse, so let's get moving!"

The blizzard set records across Nebraska. It raged so long that I got used to it. The dog was starting to recover.

I soaked her paws in warm water and rubbed the ice out of her coat and got her warmed up. I gave her two hot dogs from the fridge and she gulped them down okay, so she had an appetite. But she was very tired, and when she'd eaten, Sadie lay down near the heat vent and went to sleep.

I sat there and watched her. A wretch of a Newfoundland, skinny and scared. The wind blew 30 below zero out there, and the dog shivered as she slept.

I reached down and petted her head.

The dog came awake and stared at the heat vent, the magic of heat and life emanating from a floor. Outside the wind moaned so desolate. God didn't blow the electricity out, and the wind finally calmed. The sun rose over a cold land, shapeless under the snow.

Sadie had looked back at her kennel. In the middle of that raging death, she had looked back at the kennel.

Sometimes it's best not to question what you do.

JOHNNY CRAZY...

48TH STREET WAS CLOSED due to construction, and Bill Edwards frowned at the orange sign. He never liked taking north 27th Street to work, because five times out of ten Johnny Crazy would be in the middle of the street, preaching what he called "The Mysteries of the Lord!"

He wasn't dangerous, that anybody knew. But he did wear a white robe and sandals, and he carried a shepherd's staff, which could be a weapon.

And he preached violently, contorting his gnarled black African face and screaming at the sky:

"Get right! Get right, People! Put love into your hearts, People, God damn you to Hell! Find the Lord, O Sinners I see walking around me, driving your cars around me. You in the blue Honda—yeah, go on by! You won't look at me, you look away! What you looking away from? Get right, you people! Or God damn you to Hell!"

Bill Edwards craned his head down 27th Street. Yeah, he was there, holding up the traffic. A black and white phantom drifting down the middle of the street, cars flowing around him like sea waves. Bill Edwards heard him crack his staff into the concrete of 27th Street. Good God, he thought. "Come on, let's go, damn you," he said at the traffic crawling ahead of him. "He's harmless, drive around him and let's go!"

Every time Bill Edwards drove past Johnny Crazy, the lunatic would stare into his car and yell belligerently—"You will know!"—his face supremely fearless, as only the mad can be.

But this time he said nothing, only stood aiming his dangerous eyes. He stood in the middle of congested 27th Street, a Negro statue in white robes and rotted sandals, carrying that staff of his, as Bill Edward's Explorer approached him.

Bill Edwards had seen people toss coins at him, and seen Johnny Crazy spit at the coins on the street, his eyes beyond any of that. He said nothing as Bill Edwards drove around him, only stared in such a strange way that Bill Edwards had to look back; and doing so, he slammed right into the car in front of him.

Tresa West shivered as her Toyota Corolla jolted suddenly, then lurched and rammed the back of the Lexus in front of her.

"Oh God!" she cried out. Then caught herself. "Oh, My God, it's a Lexus!"

She glanced into the rearview mirror at the Ford Explorer that had rammed into the back of her car. The man sat there in shock. Cars began creeping around them, horns honking, people staring. Beyond in the rearview mirror was the crazy guy in the middle of the street, swinging his white robes at the sky.

The man in front of her, driving the expensive Lexus, didn't seem hurt. He climbed out of the car and came up to her window. "We'd better get these damn things over to the curb," he said. "Then call the police."

"All right," she said. She was in control, but her voice sounded funny to her, shaken up.

"It was that guy's fault," you know," he said.

"Yes, I know."

The man, fifty-five or so, a businessman or doctor, or wealthy lawyer, strutted back to his car and eased it over to the curb. The man who had caused this appeared suddenly at her window.

"My God, I'm sorry!" he said. "I was looking back at that mad man, and I—ma'am, I am so sorry. This is all my fault. Are you okay?"

"You caused me to hit that car." She nodded at the Lexus. "Yes, I'm okay."

"I know, and I'm sorry. I will take full responsibility."

"Well, we should get out of this traffic, if we can," she said.

He looked at her for the first time. She was pretty. But how could he think of that at a time like this? A damned disaster, and all because 48th Street just happened to be closed, and Johnny Crazy had to be out distracting traffic, causing wrecks. Where are the damned police when you really need them? Like clearing crazy menaces off 27th Street?

No, you can't blame him, you caused this wreck. She is pretty... "We should," he said. "Get out of the traffic."

"I think that man in the Lexus is calling the police."

"Oh." He frowned at her.

"So we'd better try and get our cars over to the curb if we can," she said.

"Of course."

The cars rolled over and formed a trio against the curb. Bill Edwards got out and wandered up to speak to the Lexus guy: "I'm sorry, Sir, this wreck was all my fault. I got distracted, I looked away, and—I'm sorry."

"Well, it's easy to get distracted with that clown out causing wrecks. Usually the police have him away by now."

Bill Edwards looked around at Johnny Crazy, standing white-robed in the middle of the street as cars flowed past him.

"No, I can't blame him," Bill Edwards said.

Tresa West got out of her car and joined them on the curb. "We can just exchange insurance cards, can't we?" she said. "It's a fender-bender, why call the police? I don't want to be late for class."

She looked at Mr. Edwards. He was a handsome man, one truly sorry for ruining a morning drive to class. She heard Johnny Crazy preaching now, against the traffic of 27th Street. Mr. Edwards was staring at her.

"They can have a look at it," the Lexus man said. "And while they're here, they can get him off the street and back to the Regional Center."

"The Regional Center?" Bill asked.

"The State madhouse. He's been there a dozen times. He doesn't get mad or violent and they let him out, warning him every time not to go out and act crazy. But here he is again, out in the middle of 27th and Vine Streets."

"Well, it was my fault. I'm sorry, Miss—?"

"West. Tresa West."

"Tresa. I'm Bill Edwards. This is a hell of a way to meet."

She smiled at him. "It is."

"Roger Currey," said the Lexus man. "You know, you could have a suit against the city, Bill."

"For what?"

"For not removing a menace from a city street. How many wrecks has that maniac caused? And the city does nothing about it. How can a maniac stand in the middle of 27th and Vine Street in an American city, and be allowed to cause that kind of danger?"

"It was me," Bill Edwards said. "I shouldn't have got distracted."

"Well, I know I'm going to be late for class," Tresa said.

Bill rubbed at his face. "I'm sorry."

"You don't have to keep saying that."

"He's made 27th and Vine the most dangerous intersection in Lincoln," Roger Currey said, staring at Johnny Crazy.

"Are you from Nebraska, Tresa?"

"No; Springfield, Missouri. I'm attending classes here at the university."

"And I've made you late for class."

"No more apologizing," she said. "Are you from Nebraska?"

"I'm afraid so. Born and raised here in Lincoln. This is the first accident I've caused since I was 16."

She laughed. "It's only a fender-bender."

"What are you interested in?"

"Bachelor of Fine Arts," she said, rather defensively.

"You'll never get anywhere with that," Roger Currey grunted. "I told my son when he went to the university here, that if I was going to pay for an education, it'd better be one that brings in a good salary."

"Did he get a degree?" Bill asked.

"No, he quit. He didn't want a degree. He works construction."

"The crazy man's staring at us," Tresa West said. "He's staring over at us."

The wraith stood in the middle of 27th and Vine, tapping his staff to the concrete. His eyes sinister, his smile lost in madness.

"He's glad he caused this wreck," Roger Currey said. "Look at the attention he's getting."

"Well, he's likely to be there, so drivers should just look out for him."

"What are you interested in?" Tresa asked him.

He stared into a beautiful flirty face. He loved her at that moment, and something took hold of him that he couldn't explain. He sensed that she felt it too. This was a crazy, supreme moment, he felt it. And she did too. Tresa gave him a long strange look. He saw deep longing in her eyes. And fear.

My God, a girl I ran in to? He smiled at her eyes. "I hope your husband won't be mad."

"I'm not married."

"Oh. Well, I hope your boyfriend…"

"I don't have a boyfriend."

"Ah. Why not? A girl as"—he looked over at Roger Currey— "pretty as you are. Why not?"

Tresa laughed. "What are you interested in, Mr. Currey?"

"I'm a businessman," Roger Currey said. "What college did you attend, Bill?"

"What makes you think I even went to college?" Bill asked. "Maybe I passed all that education and went on to better things."

"You have the college way of speaking."

"That's true," Bill said. "And I can't drive a car without ramming into people and screwing up the day. Telltale sign of too much college."

"It's the madman's fault. Standing in the middle of a public street causing accidents."

"No, I'm the one at fault," Bill said.

"You're a teacher," Tresa said. "I've seen you walking across campus."

"That's where I spend most of my time."

"Are you a professor?" Roger Currey demanded.

"I'm afraid so."

"All right. I told my son that the university could become a dreamworld that wants to keep you, even though you know you should go out there. In business college, we had a name for it, Bill." Roger Currey leaned over and whispered into his ear: "Sucking on the tit too long."

"All right."

"What do you teach?" Tresa asked, breaking up the whisper.

"Physics," Bill said.

"Science, eh?"

"Yes. So, you're a businessman, Mr. Currey."

"I got an M.A. in Business Administration, from the University of Nebraska, 1969. So you teach, Bill."

"I also do research."

"What kind of research?"

"Chaos Theory," Bill said. "Ironically, just what happened this morning, I'm sorry to say."

"What is your wife going to say about this accident?" Tresa asked.

"I don't have a wife. I'm not married."

"Your girlfriend, then."

"I'm afraid I don't have a girlfriend. I've been busy. In fact, this disaster I've caused has ruined a lot of good time in the lab."

"In the lab." Tresa smiled sadly at him.

"That means at the computer."

"Well, it sounds like a well-paying career," Roger Currey said. "But—as I told my son—teaching at a university is a dead-end job. Your insurance rates are going to go up because of this, but I still say you have a good case against the city. That crazy Negro man shouldn't be allowed to stand in a street in America and spout out."

"He's not really hurting anybody," Bill said.

"I don't care about my car," said Roger Currey. "It's that I had a bear sitting on the passenger side, and the bear got smashed and dirty when my car was rammed."

"A bear?"

"Yes, a stuffed bear. I keep it on the passenger side of the car always. It was a stuffed bear that my grand daughter invited to our tea party."

"Tea party," Tresa West said.

"Long ago, when she was very little. Mr. Bear, he was called. Now my grand daughter's—eighteen, I believe. And the crash tore the—I'm sounding foolish, aren't I?"

"Was she your son's daughter?" Bill asked.

"She was. I haven't seen her in a long time. Her name is Sarah."

"Maybe you should see her," Tresa said.

"I've got a meeting at nine-thirty. And it's a quarter to nine now."

"I've got a class I'll miss," Tresa said.

"I will too," Bill said. "You probably like intellectual movies?"

She looked at him. "What?"

"Films that show human nature. You probably wouldn't want to see a science fiction action film or something like that."

"I could surprise you. Girls from Missouri do that."

He smiled. "If the cops don't haul me away, I would love to make this fender-bender right and buy you dinner—and a sci-fi movie."

"You might be surprised to know that I like sci-fi movies. And Chinese food."

"My favorite," Bill Edwards said.

"Dating a student was never allowed in the College of Business Administration," Roger Currey remarked.

"Man, look at him," Bill said, staring at Johnny Crazy out there in the middle of the street. "Look at him dancing away."

"What would make a man do that day after day, knowing everyone on God's green earth is laughing at him, and knowing they're going to drag him back to the Regional Center? It's almost as if he's *absorbing* the laughter. Always 27th and Vine, and always yelling out like a prophet. Always getting into peoples' faces and yelling at them. What gives him the right?"

"Don't you want to see your grand daughter?" Bill asked.

Roger Currey looked at him. "It's been a very long time."

"Why?"

"I don't know. There was never time. Now there's this time and I just thought about her, that's all."

"He gave us time." Bill smiled at Tresa. Then he smiled at the crazy wraith dancing in the middle of 27th and Vine, Johnny Crazy grinning black-and-white at them: "Know the truth, Brothers and Sisters! See the Truth!"—morning sun flashing gold in his teeth:

"I am no saint, I am no prophet, I am an Angel! And those that can see will know it! Those that have eyes will see!"

"He's the one who made this wreck," Roger Currey said. "No one should have the right to stand in the middle of the street and cause wrecks."

"What was she like?" Tresa asked. "Your grand daughter."

"She was a little chipmunk—beautiful. My son's daughter." Roger Currey stared around at the neighborhood. "She only lives a few blocks from here."

"You could go visit her, after all this."

"I haven't seen her in— years. I'm busy, I have a lot of things to do. I'm not used to getting into wrecks and waiting for the police. I have a meeting. My God, look at that traffic."

"Everybody wanting to get to work."

"I could stop over, see how she's doing," Roger Currey said. "After all this."

Bill looked back at Johnny Crazy in the middle of 27th and Vine, yelling into car windows, pounding on the cars that he was an angel. Are angels that crazy?

"Here's the police," Tresa said, looking down 27th Street. "Finally."

"I hope they haul that—no, I don't." Roger Currey looked down the street. "After this, I think I'll pay my grand daughter a visit, see how she's doing."

"You don't expect an angel to be bellowing into a car window at you," Bill said, staring at the squad cars and policemen converging at 27th and Vine, making a nightmare of traffic. "Or standing staring at you until you have to cause a wreck."

"No, you don't expect that," Tresa said. "I didn't expect it."

"I didn't either."

"I am the angel!" Johnny Crazy yelled out, smiling at the policemen, who went through the routine of hand-cuffing him and leading him away to the Regional Center.

Johnny Crazy stared at the traffic squirreling around him.

"I am the angel of 27th Street!" he cried.

"I wonder if he's crazy," Roger Currey said.

"What do you mean?"

"I'm not sure. Only that I think when the police are through with us, I'll drive up and see how my grand daughter's doing."

Bill Edwards looked at Tresa West. "Well? Fantastic Four, Rise of the Silver Surfer? Come on. Then a late dinner."

She laughed. Then she looked over at Johnny Crazy and stopped smiling. "They're taking him off to the state hospital."

"I don't think it'll do much good. He's really harmless, if you learn to drive around him."

"And not listen to him?"

"I always listened to him."

Bill Edwards stared at Johnny Crazy scooting into the police car. Johnny Crazy stared out, and Bill Edwards saw those mad eyes, staring straight at him. "You see, don't you?" Johnny Crazy yelled.

THE SUIT...

MARTIN PILLROY WAS ONE of the greatest metallurgists the world has ever known. He was also a tormented 35 year old who had never been on a date. He understood metals, alloys, elements...he had never understood girls—women—them.

He stared into the mirror that stood tall and majestic and gold-bordered in his expensive living room that a battalion of decorators had created. The mirror reflected his vast techno-fortress of solitude, out on a forgotten Nebraska farm.

Am I going insane?

A skinny, balding, scared man looked back.

Childhood—particularly high school childhood—had carved deep, unhealed scars into Martin Pillroy. Twenty years later his mind couldn't get rid of those guys: the athletes who'd pushed him around so relentlessly, like a cowardly doll. Slapping his face and washing his hair in the toilet, and making him crawl on the high school floor.

They recognized a skinny genius, a pimpled pocket-calculator. They tortured him; they humiliated him in front of giggling girls. They *knew* that his life would mean more than theirs. He would do more than they ever could—make more money, succeed and conquer!

And they never would.

But he did. At the age of 28 Martin Pillroy patented the new substance of the age, a carbon alloy—Sterion— that contained a secret that cannot to this day be known.

Twenty million dollars later Martin Pillroy darted away from the scientific world, into a fortress farm in Nebraska, 20 miles west of Lincoln.

Only, it wasn't really a fortress; it wasn't really a farm or a home.

It was a laboratory designed to build a super hero.

"How pathetic," Martin said, turning away from the mirror. All the work he had done in the last three years seemed no more than a dream. And dreams are either wonderful stories—or terrifying ones. But only stories. It's one thing to write a story, but another to truly create one.

A fierce, featherlight skeleton reacting to a super-battery, all enclosed in super-carbon, its copper nerves begging for electricity, its plastic veins tight with hydraulic fluid, its mini-computer driving electricity, power and speed into the structure…a co-dependant form that was at this stage very difficult to control.

He looked around him at the walls of comic books that defined his living room; a comic book collection of several hundred.

The comic books.

They had saved him after Don Steiner, the football hero, tripped him in the hall that day. He had been looking at Sarah Simmons, the cheerleader; then Don Steiner tripped him and he fell spilling his books across the high school hallway and tumbling down to his skinny knees.

They all laughed at him scrumbling to get his books. Everybody laughed—Sarah Simmons laughed. And Martin Pillroy learned how to draw the dark blanket of his mind around him.

The comic books saved him after that. The super heroes saved him.

He looked across his living room at the door to his workroom, the domain that had taken hours, days, weeks, years from him.

The Suit.

He thought of Laura Lender, a pretty technician who worked at American Graphite, the corporation he had enriched then escaped. How she would smile at him often, and make shy suggestions of romance.

Martin Pillroy, ever the mouse, had always scampered back into the shadows of his mind, seeing fear everywhere out there.

Even after his triumph with Sterion, and with money flooding over him from everywhere, the mouse won and the super hero lost.

That time.

He stared into the mirror. You couldn't even find the courage to ask her out to dinner.

It's time to change. The super hero never loses.

He climbed into the sterion suit and activated its computer system. He charged up, feeling the prickle of energy in the battery pack that was spread across his lower torso.

Sensors flickered on. He flexed his sterion arms and felt the superhydrolic blood filling them. He sneered at life and clicked the control bracelet on his wrist to ten. At the highest level of the suit, one twitch of the arm was a piston exploding from his plated shoulder.

A test slab of reinforced concrete sat before him. Those bullies, those cold-hearted monsters of high school sat before him, their cruel eyes cursing him forever.

His fist shot into the concrete slab, and it exploded to frags, bent re-bar and dust.

It was like striking sand. Martin Pillroy retracted the arm; it had moved faster than thought. He studied the powerful fist. Concrete dust, not a scratch.

Time to experiment. Time to take it for a test drive.

He thought of Laura. He thought of his own hateful cowardice. He stared at the walls of comic books, the super heroes who'd given him a strange door to hope.

He stared back at the mirror. "It's time?" he asked.

The guy in the jogging outfit was doing some kind of yoga out here in the dark. It was friggin one o'clock in the morning, this was Antelope Park, and in the parklight this guy was going through these moves…a weird guy—his head looked too small for his body; well, it didn't matter. His wrist flashed silver in the park lights, and he was wearing a rich guy's outfit. Chances are he had a wallet with something in it.

Darius Jones stepped out of the trees. "Hey, Man!" he said. "I need to get paid."

Martin Pillroy stared at the man, appearing from the darkness. A nightmare. His throat tried to swallow. "I'm just testing something," he said. "That's all."

"Okay, that's fine," Darius said. "But now I need to get paid. You know what I mean?"

Martin Pillroy stared in fright. "No."

Darius Jones drew a knife from his coat. A splinter of steel flashed in the moonlight. "Give me your watch and your wallet and you won't get hurt. You understand?"

Martin Pillroy's stomach was sick. "No, this isn't a watch! It's a monitor…"

"I don't care what it is, give it to me." The man strutted up at him. "I need to get paid."

The man and the knife charged at him.

Martin Pillroy did not know if he reacted or the suit did. But his left arm shot out, striking the man's hand, shattering the wrist and spinning the knife away.

"Ahhh!" The mugger grabbed his wrist and stumbled back in disbelief.

High school was suddenly unleashed: A tormentor was now staring at *Him* in terror.

Martin went after the mugger: the suit formed a fist and it suddenly shot out and exploded into the man's face, shattering it like an egg.

Blood blasted the night. The man made a noise, buckled to the grass and it was all over. Martin Pillroy, speckled with blood and brain, stood in horror over the corpse.

His mind reeled, his heart chattered. Oh, God…

I have killed another human being. Martin couldn't look down at the man. He turned and escaped, scrambling out of the park and back to his Lexus.

"He tried to attack somebody with this knife," Detective Dickerson said.

"Somebody." Detective Emerson stared down at the corpse. "Man, I feel sick."

"The guy broke his wrist with a baseball bat, then went to work on the face."

"It looks that way. Or a tire iron, or a pipe. That's a pretty rotten face."

The sun was glinting beyond Lincoln, another day growing. A yellow-red-black morning crept over the trees in Antelope Park.

The coroner was arriving, other squad cars, and red-blue-white sparkles. No sirens, but sparkles in the dark dawn.

Dickerson looked down at the corpse. "Darius Jones. Sorry to see you again, Da-ri-us. How you doing? Not so good, I see."

Emerson frowned. His partner had a disturbing habit of talking to the murder victims, to the dead. But if it helped solve the crime, what the hell.

"You ripped off the wrong people," Dickerson said. "They caught you in this park, you pulled out your skinny knife, and they made potato salad of your face."

"I don't know," Emerson said. "Darius wasn't so stupid."

"A drug addict and a mugger? How much more stupid do you need?"

"Not stupid enough to get caught like this. Does it look like he tried to run?"

Dickerson studied the scene. The coroner's people were shuffling down the hill now, other cops. Dickerson heard their scrambling footsteps.

"No, he pulled out his knife and tried to fight back."

"Does that sound like Darius Jones? He wouldn't fight back, not with a knife, not with a machine gun. He'd run."

"Unless he was cornered and desperate."

"I don't know." Emerson stared at the sun, the dawn too bright, scarlet and yellow. "This seems kind of weird to me."

"Me too." Dickerson stared down at the murder victim, the splintered wrist and crushed face. "I don't know either. Tell me about this, Darius. It's starting to not make sense. Come on, talk to me, Man."

Martin Pillroy had put on the suit, and it had committed murder. He would never put on the suit again.

Martin sat in his robe and thought about eating something for breakfast—but he was sick to his stomach. He tried to get that horrible thing out of his mind: that fist going off like a shotgun, blowing that man's face into a canyon. It couldn't have happened—but he knew it had.

"Never again. The super hero suit has been tested—and my God…"

Martin Pillroy looked into the tall mirror in the living room. "The man tried to kill me! I was doing nothing wrong, and the man drew a knife on me and tried to kill me. I fought back. Finally, I fought back."

"No more." Martin looked away from the mirror. "Sell it to the Pentagon. Twenty-five million, it's worth that."

"It's worth 25—" Martin stared back into the mirror. Beyond his reflection he saw the walls of comic books. He remembered every feverish second he had spent with them.

There in Antelope Park he had been terrified—and then suddenly he had not been terrified. There in Antelope Park, in Lincoln, Nebraska, he had fought back.

"I fought back!" he yelled at the mirror.

You murdered a man, the mirror said.

"I was a super hero!"

The mirror stared. Do you want to be a super hero, or do you want to marry Laura? You love her—you fear her—you fear everything.

"No!" Martin said. "I *was* a super hero."

No. The suit was a super hero, not you. Sell this technology to the government, make millions of dollars and marry Laura. That's the way to happiness—for Martin Pillroy.

"I already have millions of dollars. And maybe I don't want happiness."

The mirror skrinched at him: Do you not? Happiness is in your hands. Laura will be your wife. The suit will bring you millions of dollars. You'd better think about it, Martin; because happiness is yours if you just take it.

"I don't believe in happiness," Martin said. "Only joy."

Joy?

"Joy and then destruction."

The suit has corrupted you.

"Yes, it has."

The mirror stared back at him for several moments. What will you name this doomed super hero?

"The Suit."

Remember this, said the mirror. The suit committed murder.

"He drove a Lexus," the old woman told the detectives. "And I tell you, he came out of the park like some Spiderman thing. And he got into that silver Lexus and he drove away."

"You're sure it was a Lexus, Ma'am," said Dickerson.

"Yes, a silver Lexus. My late husband sold them for the last ten years of his life. It was a silver Lexus. Well anyway, Princess barked out that she had to go poop." The old woman smiled fondly at the tiny terrier dog getting underfoot. "I took Princess out to do her business, and that was when I saw that strange creature. And then when I heard about the murder on 10/11, well…"

"What exactly seemed strange about him?" Dickerson asked.

"I'm not sure. The way he moved. It was like when I watch one of these new movies with my grandchildren, and the special effects make the man move somehow jerky and not real."

"All right, Ma'am," Emerson said. "Thank you for your time."

"One man killed him?" Dickerson said. "A guy driving a Lexus."

"Could be Roberto, or his fellows."

"Could be." Dickerson stared at Antelope Park. "Why am I getting a strange thing about this?"

"I don't know," Emerson said. "But I am too."

He almost hoped to get her voice mail. But Laura picked up, and he heard that far-off familiar voice.

"Hi, Laura," he said. "It's—well, it's Martin...Pillroy?"

"Martin! My God, we've been wondering all over about you," she said.

"About me?"

"You disappeared. Where are you? What are you doing?"

"Well, Laura—presently I'm in Nebraska. I've been doing some research...do you like steak?"

"What, Martin?"

"Steak and baked potato and fresh garden salad? I would recommend Dorothy Lynch Salad Dressing, it's the best. I have a plane ticket for you."

A pause. "Are you all right, Martin?"

"All right?"

"You disappeared for almost 3 years. What are you doing, Martin, are you okay?"

"Yes." He stared away for a moment. "However, I'd like to invite you to dinner, to the Steak House in Lincoln. Don't worry, I'll pay for everything. Unless you're married or your boyfriend..."

"What?"

Martin took a long drink of air. "I'm only asking if you'll have dinner with me, Laura—that's all. If you don't want to..."

"I do want to, Martin," her voice said in the phone.

He was not in the suit, but he was in its essence. He remembered the power that grabbed his body.

"I'm sorry I never asked you out to dinner before," he said. "I always meant to. I was afraid. Now I'm not afraid."

"A Nebraska beef steak," her voice said. "Baked potato and salad. I'd love to have that dinner with you, Martin. And you can tell me what you've been up to."

Emerson pulled into the handi-capped space outside of Duggin's Pub. Night scags lingered about: lonely rags, old half-dead hippies, bar crawlers.

The big biker in the denim vest sat on the curb grunting in pain.

Dickerson just got out of the patrol car when an old grey drunk grabbed his coat.

"Hey, man!"

"I saw the guy that did it!" the drunk said. "I saw the whole thing."

"Okay," Dickerson said. "So lay your hands off me."

"This guy rolls up here on a honey-bee yellow Kawasaki, a crotch-rocket. He parks it right next to this old guy's Harley."

"That guy over there," Dickerson said.

"The Harley guy's drunk, and see how big he is? The Kawasaki guy kind of walks like a dink. But there's something weird about him."

"Weird like how?"

"I don't know. There was a strange, crooked strut to how he walked. So the Harley guy tells the dink to get his Jap-crap bike off the street. The dink—he's wearing this real puffy jogging outfit—stands there and explains to that drunk biker that he's parked in a legal place!" The grey drunk sprayed out a laugh, and Dickerson frowned and backed away.

"That's how the fight started?" he asked. "That guy didn't like the other guy's brand of motorcycle."

"Yeah, that's it. Well, here's the crazy part: the big biker over there took a swing at this dink, and I thought there goes the dink's head; but then the dink's arm shot out, and he caught that old boy's swinging fist in his hand. The Harley guy's so stupefied that he swings his left. The dink catches that one, then he crushes both of that guys fists. I could hear bone crunch all the way over here. It sounded like crushing a bag of potato chips!"

Dickerson looked over at his partner, who was interviewing the big ugly biker with the shattered hands. Now the sirens from Bryan West Hospital startled the night.

"That guy's hands are like broken pretzels," Emerson said.

"Yeah, they are."

They pulled out of the Pub and took 13ᵗʰ Street south where the grey drunk had said the dink on the yellow crotch rocket had escaped.

"Yellow Kaw, that loud; shouldn't be too hard to find."

"I don't know, Man." Dickerson stared out at the streets of Lincoln. Two in the morning, and the neighborhoods quiet, sleeping, dark.

Broken pretzels.

"This is really strange," Emerson said at last.

"Tell me about it. I never would have believed that old hippie and his kung-fu shit story."

"The Biker said it was like his fists were in hydraulic presses. He works manufacturing, so he knows about hydraulic presses. He tried to clock the little guy twice, and the Kaw guy caught his fists like a snake catches a rat, and crushed them to—what you saw."

"What I saw ain't going to work manufacturing or anything else," Dickerson said. "What do we got here, partner?"

"I don't know." Emerson peered round at the dark neighborhoods just north of A Street. "Some ninja warrior?"

"I keep thinking about what happened to Darius," Dickerson said.

Emerson frowned. "Me too."

"Laura, I'm not very expressive." Martin Pillroy started his speech when they had settled in at the Steak House. "I've always been unsuccessful talking to women." He grabbed a napkin from the table for no reason whatsoever.

"Martin, you are who you are," Laura said. "And I've always loved you for who you are."

Martin Pillroy's stomach turned over, and electro-magnetism shuddered up his spine. His heart bloomed. He thought of the workroom, in the secret cavern of his house; he thought of the golden mirror. He smiled. He felt powerful, fearless: "I had a speech memorized for you, Laura," he said. "But speeches are for cowards. I'm not a coward anymore, Laura."

She stared at him. "What are you saying, Martin?"

He looked down at the table. "I don't know, exactly."

"You look tired, Martin," Laura said. "Everybody at AG is placing bets on what you've been working on."

Martin stared up at her. "What do you mean?"

"Well, everybody knows you're working on something incredible, Martin."

"Something that would no doubt make me richer."

Laura's face fell: "Martin, I know that you're a genius. If you make money, all right. If you don't make any money, that's all right too. I love you, Martin. You may be complicated, but it's that simple: I love you."

Martin studied her. "No matter what I am?"

"No matter," she said.

Martin waited until the waitress had brought their steaks, breadsticks, baked potato, salad and drinks, then trotted away.

"What if I'm a super hero?" he asked across the table. Martin's stomach rolled. No! Don't tell her that! It has to be a dead secret.

"What?" She stared at him.

"Just kidding." He began sawing into his luscious Nebraska steak. He smiled at Laura. He was no longer Martin Pillroy, he was The Suit. "I love you, Laura," he said fearlessly. "And I'm asking you to marry me."

His security system went off at two o'clock in the morning. Martin in pajamas stumbled out of bed and stumbled across the living room and peered into the front door eye-hole. A knock on the door scared him, and he flinched back.

"Dr. Pillroy?" a voice called from beyond the oaken door. "Dr. Pillroy, we're sorry to disturb you at this hour. We're detectives from the Lincoln Police Department. We just want to ask you a few questions."

Martin Pillroy was sick. "What?"

"Dr. Pillroy, we just want to ask you a couple of questions; then we'll be gone."

"All right."

He unlocked the door, and these two men came in, displaying badges. Martin offered them chairs in the living room. They both looked over at the door to his workroom.

"It's the middle of the night," he said, blinking at them.

"Yeah, sorry," Detective Dickerson said. He rested down in the thousand dollar living room sofa that Martin had wanted to impress

Laura with. "I don't sleep very good." Dickerson looked at him. "My partner here says I'm a born night-crawler."

Martin scrambled into the living room. "What can I—what can I help you with, officers?"

Dickerson looked over at the door to the workroom. He studied it for some time. "A guy got his hands crushed night before last, outside the Pub in Lincoln."

"What?"

"A week earlier," Emerson spoke up. "A guy's head was crushed in Antelope Park."

"I saw that on the 10/11 News," Martin said.

"Well, a witness saw a silver Lexus screech away from Antelope Park that night," Dickerson said. "And a witness saw a honey-bee yellow Kawasaki 1200 crotch-rocket screech away from the thing at the Pub."

"I don't understand," Martin said.

"Well, you have a silver Lexus and a honey-bee yellow Kawasaki crotch-rocket, that's all."

"But I never take—look here, what are you saying?"

"Nothing," Emerson said. "We're just asking."

"Asking what?"

"Where you were," Dickerson said. "At about one-thirty in the morning on June 12th."

"June 12th?"

"Last Saturday."

"I was here," Martin said. "I hardly ever go out. I stay at home."

"With a 1200 crotch rocket in the garage?" Dickerson questioned.

"I take it out sometimes, to blow out the pipes. That's all. Gentlemen, I'm a scientist. Look at me: could I be a murderer?"

Emerson frowned. "Nobody said anything about murder, Dr. Pillroy."

"No, but—look at me! Could I do these things you're talking about?"

Dickerson traded faces with his partner. Emerson frowned back at him.

"Who knows?"

"No more," he said to the mirror.

You're scared, Martin.

"I am! I'm scared! God, God, God what have I done?"

You're scared of courage.

"I'm scared of prison."

You weren't scared of that villain who attacked you in Antelope Park; or that bully who attacked you—

"But enough is enough." Martin Pillroy stared into the gilt mirror.

Is it?

"Yes! I was a super hero."

You don't look like a super hero, said the mirror. Martin Pillroy will always be afraid; the Suit will never be afraid.

"Those police detectives—they know!"

They only suspect. They had no search warrant, you didn't have to let them in.

"If Laura finds out—"

That you've created a super hero?

"I want to marry her."

And she wants to marry you.

Martin glanced around at the door to the workroom, the Suit. "I didn't fear anymore," he muttered to himself.

For your money, the mirror said behind him. She wants to marry you for your money, nothing else.

"No. For me. She wants to marry me for me, for who I am."

Who are you? The mirror asked. Martin Pillroy, or the Suit?

The house's alarm system blared out, and Martin shuddered in fear. He stared at the front door, expecting a nightmare. He scampered over and peered out the peephole

Detective Dickerson.

Martin flung open the door. "It's the middle of the night!" he cried.

"I know." Dickerson gave him a tired, apologetic face. "Please forgive me, Dr. Pillroy. Can I come in?"

"Yes," Martin Pillroy frowned. "Please, come in."

"Thank you." Dickerson trudged into the living room and collapsed onto the five thousand dollar couch that framed the ten thousand dollar fireplace. He gave Martin a look of instant mutual understanding. He smiled: "You need to quit, Dr. Pillroy."

Martin fumbled himself into a chair. "What?"

"What you're doing. You need to quit."

"I don't understand."

"No, I don't either. But you need to quit it." Dickerson gave him a smile that was almost reptilian, eyelids hooded in the lamplight: "A silver Lexus and a honey-bee yellow Kaw 1200. A scientific genius, who acts really guilty…"

"I—don't understand," Martin stammered.

"Sure you do." Dickerson smiled at him. "This last one nailed you to the wall, Dr. Pillroy. Three nights ago? Outside the alley on 13th Street?"

Martin stared at the police detective. He remembered it, but only as a dream: wandering down the alley in the Suit, toward the red neon Wells Fargo sign. There, in the quiet Lincoln street, a guy was slapping his girlfriend. She screamed out as her boyfriend whipped his hand savagely across her face, and Martin Pillroy acted. He stepped out of the neon alley and tore into the boyfriend, smashing his face, sending him to the concrete.

The girl had screamed, and stared at him in horror. "Jesus, you Bastard!" she screamed at him. "Get out of here!"

"Guy that ran away from that fight," Dickerson said to him. "He was riding the yellow Kaw. The girlfriend saw him ride away."

Martin stared at the detective. "The girlfriend."

"Yeah, who this guy tried to save. Only he couldn't save her, because she didn't want to be saved."

"I don't know what any of this has to do with me," Martin said.

Dickerson smiled at him. "It has everything to do with you, Dr. Pillroy. Quit what you're doing, right now. You got a lot of money, you got a nice palace out here. You got everything you need, Dr. Pillroy. I've been told that you can make any kind of money you want with your mind."

Martin Pillroy looked at Detective Dickerson. He felt almost unconscious, as if the world was swimming in mist. "Did you read comics when you were young?"

Dickerson smiled. "That's what got me into law enforcement."

"I saw you looking my collection over." Martin stared around at the gilt-mirror. "What's wrong with a super hero?" he asked.

Dickerson stared away. "What's wrong is that the super hero stops the boyfriend from beating up the girlfriend—then the girlfriend winds up loving the boyfriend more and hating the super hero and pressing charges. What's wrong is, the super hero goes to prison and the boyfriend goes back to slapping his girlfriend."

"It's not supposed to be that way."

"No, probably not." Detective Dickerson studied the walls of comic books: "I don't have a collection like this. But I'll bet I've read most of these comics. And I'll bet you can't name any super hero or super villain that I don't know—intimately."

"The world needs a super hero."

Dickerson looked at him. "There are two kinds of super hero: The ones who become super heroes in an accident, a twist of fate. Like falling into a vat of chemicals, or stumbling into gamma rays, or being bitten by a radioactive bug, or being from another planet. They didn't choose or want to be super heroes.

"The ones I liked the best were the others, the ones who *made* themselves super heroes. Batman, Ironman—normal destructible humans who made themselves super heroes. Because they *wanted* to be a super hero. I liked them the best."

"Why?"

"Well, because they didn't cheat. Destiny didn't make them super heroes, they made themselves, with their hands and their minds. They weren't *accidental* super heroes."

Martin was studying the detective. "You've been investigating me."

"Oh, yes, Dr. Pillroy. Dr. Martin Pillroy, the creator of Sterion. Eccentric, reclusive, rumored to be working on a secret military project."

"That's untrue," Martin said. "You're not making any sense." He stood up. "Now, I think you should leave, Detective Dickerson."

Dickerson got up from the silken couch. He startled the scientist by suddenly clutching Martin's arm and squeezing it. "Stop it, Martin," he whispered.

"Wha—?"

"Quit." Detective Dickerson stared into his eyes. "I don't want to see my favorite kind of super hero in prison."

Martin glanced over at the door to his workroom. "What if he can't quit? What if the power won't let him?"

Dickerson looked over at the door to the workroom. He grunted. "Those comic books are all about power, aren't they? That's why nerdy kids like us ate them up. Because we had no power. Having special powers, and using them for good, or bad. That's the comic books.

"But you know, Dr. Pillroy, what the true power of super heroes is? Not super strength or invisibility or the ability to shoot out rays or walk through walls. That's not the real power of super heroes."

"What are you saying?"

"The real power of super heroes is that they're not real. They are stories more true because they're not true. You have a girlfriend, Dr. Pillroy."

Martin gave him a startled look.

"Marry her, be happy—quit. I don't want to see a super hero go to prison."

Martin's stomach queased. He fought back nausea. "I will," he promised. "I will stop."

"Good."

Martin stared out the window until the police detective's car was gone. Then he turned to the golden mirror in the living room.

"You heard him—no more!" he said. "This is the end. The Suit is no more!"

How can you go back? The mirror quietly asked him.

Martin stared around at the door to his workroom.

How can you ever go back?

A ROOT CANAL...

I T USED TO DEPRESS me that people are such dribbling idiots.

But wait. I've gone through an ordeal, and I have the right to say that.

I had emergency oral surgery done oh, a while back: A Major Root Canal. Surgical work that sucked greeny-yellowy goblins of pus out of my exploded face and left me sweat-tense, a punctured mask in a padded chair, ugly, mortal, shaken...

Just kidding. The operation was a lot easier and less painful than I ever thought, and I actually walked out of the clinic wearing a droopy mouth smile.

It *was* semi-emergency surgery, I reasoned. Unlikely—but possibly—life-threatening. Enough, anyway, for me to let them know at work the dangerous situation I was in, claim *earned* sick-time, and then lay as protoplasm on my couch, smoke too many cigarettes and sip whiskey out of the living side of my mouth.

The Oral Surgeon suggested Ibruprophen for a "possible dull ache" that might occur while I was recuperating, when the Novocaine wore off.

I'm sorry, my learned friend. This demonic absessed toothling, and the struggle to destroy the monster gives me every legal right to recover on the couch and get drunk on whiskey, for—?

"Oh, you should rest up half a day. Or a day, if you're feeling especially achy on that side."

"So, a few days of rest."

"Oh, maybe a couple."

"A few days. Thank you, Doctor."

I had no intention of testing the Ibruprophen against whiskey. I made a domain of pillows and blankets on the couch, slid the coffee table right up so that the whiskey and coke were less than a grunt away, north of my hand; the cigarettes, Bic lighter and stone ashtray gathered south. I had wickedly turned off my cell phone, and the t.v. remote was cradled under my arm like a naked girl.

I began my recovery by smoking two big bowls of pot. Pot is smoked by cancer patients, recovering from treatment. This was close enough.

As life started to fizz again into my cheek, as the novocaine sizzled away, I got drunk and stoned and watched Alfred Hitchcock's *REAR WINDOW* . I saw me as the Jimmy Stewart character, forced on the couch by fate to recover from an operation—less Stewart's adventurous career, and of course, Grace Kelly.

Don't start judging: Stewart spent his recovery window-peeking on his neighbors. So I decided to window peek on all of America. By God, I decided to squint into the window of America.

"Television is a shit hole!" my father used to roar out.

I'm almost 57 years old, and this was way back when television wasn't anything like a shit hole. Yet it threatened books.

"You want to spend your whole life staring at a glass screen?" he would lecture us, always rhetorically.

I never told him back that he spent his life staring at paper pages. It crossed my mind, but in saying it I would have had a hardbound Ray Bradbury smashed across my mouth and his shoe punched up my ass. Mom wouldn't object, and would probably get a slap of her own in, burning my mouth. She was also a reading addict, and she loved to read the most gruesome and Satanic stories ever told. Mom devoured True Detective magazines and True Crime books, filling her spare time with the pages of serial killers and mass murderers, savage rape and unimaginable torture. And then she lectured me about spending dimes on pinball machines when I could be buying comic books.

Dad devoured science fiction—it was his way out. Books were the family hero and the television set the family villain. So I was never exposed to it the way my peers were.

Poor me. I was denied the wonderful screen by cruel, book-addicted parents.

That gives me permission, forty years later, don't you see, to sprawl like a dazed slug and stare at the same wicked devil screen, and rule it by pushing my finger.

Dad always warned us that people who read books are blessed, and people who stare at screens are cursed. Self-evident ignoramuses. The robots his science fiction novels warned him about.

"Shut off that damn thing!" he would roar at our 1959 television set.

Unless it was the Twilight Zone. Then he would sit with us and stare with us at the crackly black-and-white episode until it was over, and had scared me and my brother to death. Then the thing went off and a dead glass face peered at the living room.

So why did we even own a t.v.?

I think it had to do with Mom's fantasy about Jack LaLane and his fitness show. How the perfect LaLane moved in that gritty black-and-white fantasy, impossibly healthy and fit and alive.

She told Dad that she had to have that show in order to stay fit. Dad nodded.

I'm sorry, I'm regressing. When you've gone through something like a root canal, maybe your life—I don't know, it might not flash before your eyes, but maybe it creeps into your thoughts.

Once in the 1960's Dad grouchily took us to see a movie at the Grand Theatre. A comedy, *CAT BALLOU.* And I caught him staring at the eternal rump of Jane Fonda riding away on that horse. That scene, and how it…well…images weren't all lost to him.

A child of books, and now my parents were dead, I wanted to explore the world they had kept me from, the world of television: Mighty Mouse, Superman, Beaver, Soupy Sales, The Green Hornet, the heroes of the all-powerful eye.

Only now it had gone far beyond that, I knew: Now unreal life-games played on pocket screens, and music and drama and suspense and special effects and hi how you doing and on screens and always on screens, and how the screens sweep like the virus Dad said they would whass up? But the screens talk to you now, the screens answer Yeah, look at this hey man Oh man. Never know the world because you're never

URNver! farfromthescreenthescreenthegreyslateeverythingthatdoeseverythingandisinyoualivenowBeelikesweepingthisvirusrealityandisinyoualivenow

Since I'm drunk and stoned and recovering from major surgery, and wandering back there, I vow in the year 2009 to explore this thing that is America, this monster that has become America: The screen. I'm too drunk now to read anyway.

My Dad worshipped books as much as he hated the screen.

"I leaves you kids so that you don't have to think anymore!" he tried to explain.

But this was a new time, and I was inspired by the whiskey and my dental experience. I didn't want some dense smelly book. I didn't really want to think anymore. I wanted drunken vegetableism, the soft carpet of television. I wanted the screen—not to worship it, Dad, but to study it.

What I found surprised me. I had expected drivel and bilgewater. I had expected great crap and little else.

But I was surprised. As I gently touched the channel-change button and stared at the images flickering in my eyes, I realized that television was not the terrible thing I'd imagined.

It was worse. My misted eyes blinked at the images as I touched the channel button, pausing now and then to be sickened by some mush of a stupid show.

I know, you're thinking that I'm some kind of pompous ass—a drug abuser, an alcoholic and tobacco smoker who is bitter at the world and thinking he's so much better because he reads.

Not true, believe me. Smoking pot isn't technically abusing drugs, so you're wrong about that one.

As for the world of reading versus the world of television—don't read any further if your eyes are like that dead screen.

Please don't.

Television is crap-food.

There are eyes and there are screens. Maybe it always was, but never before was it more apparent.

Mom and Dad were addicted to books. In each their own way they went into books to get out of the world for awhile. Is the screen worse than the page? Is it any different?

Why are you asking me; I'm drunk and stoned.

WITNESS PROTECTION...

I CRINGE WHEN THE phone chatters. It's like taking a hot shower to calm down, to calm down— then suddenly the hot water runs out and ice spray hits me.

I shouldn't even have a phone, but that would be dangerously stupid.

I answer before the tiny robot can chatter again: "Hello?"

"John, this is Lieutenant Sharpe. Listen to me. There was some kind of leak, we just found out about it, we're sending officers from Lincoln PD, they should be at your house in 20 minutes—"

"What!" I feel like throwing up.

"No, stay calm. Stay in your house."

"What is this?"

A chilling pause. "They found out your new name. They know where you live."

"Oh, God."

"And they might know the police are on their way."

Oh, God. It was something my eyes saw by mistake one night:

My brain blinks back two years. Manny Sandoval, the king cobra of Detroit, in the courtroom, in his crisp, expensive suit, his eyes dark and fatal; a warning, then after I stood up and spoke, a curse. After he'd been sentenced to life in prison on my testimony, what I'd seen him do on my way home from work. I wanted to be a hero, do the right thing, show courage and step forward to say the truth. So on...

At that point I became non-existent. Not a plant foreman, I could never be that again. Not Anthony Blazio, I could never be him again. Not after Sandoval stared at me with his dark eyes and slid his finger across his throat, cutting my old life away from me.

"John, talk to me," Sharpe's voice in the phone.

"You said I'd be safe. You promised—"

"I know. Stay in your house and wait for the police."

The phone dies. I go wobbling to the desk drawer and fumble out the .38 pistol I've never shot. I never taught myself how to shoot it. I'd never dared to pull its trigger.

Oh, Jesus. Oh, God. You have to do it quick—learn how to pull the trigger.

I tremble open the chamber, though I know it's loaded. Oh, God. I snap the chamber shut.

I try to think: get into a corner and hide. Wait for the police.

Lincoln Nebraska glitters outside the window. I stare out there at the quiet dark; I twist the shades closed. Okay, 20 minutes.

I hear a sound. Something—some thing outside whispers. I shut off the light. I crawl into the darkest corner of the living room, curl myself into the shadows. I hear gruff whispers. I know they're out there, and not the police.

Oh, God.

I finger the pistol, loaded with snub-nose bullets. Can I fire it into a living being? Can I fire it at all?

Something scrapes, jiggles, snaps my door open. One, more of Sandoval's men, masters of execution. They've been watching. They have ways to know what the police know. I should never have said what I saw. Wanting to be brave, I destroyed myself. I never should have stood up in the courtroom.

Oh God, Oh God. Where are the sirens?

The .38 Special feels unreal in my hands. A strange, heavy machine. I take breaths and listen to the quiet footsteps. I squat in the dark as far as my knees let me. Oh, God.

Where are the sirens, the police?

Manny Sandoval, Lord of Detroit. A creature with power beyond my understanding. Power beyond prison. I remember his thick finger going across his thick throat as he stared at me.

They're whispering to each other now, as I crouch like a mouse.

Deep low voices, urgent and cold: "Get it done quick, the cops are on the way."

Where are the police?

Why did I give away my life to testify in court? They used me, and now they don't care if I live or not. Protective Custody, we'll take care of you.

No.

But Manfred Sandoval cares. He wants to kill me, he needs to. Oh, Christ.

The pistol feels like dead lead in my hands. Now I hear them stepping around my house, soon to find me and shoot me and slither away into the darkness.

God…where are the police?

Now I see big shadows wandering my carpet. I wanted to do right, be the hero. Now is the time to be a hero. But I can't. Fear chokes me and I only want help.

Oh God, Oh God.

Thug-shaped forms. I can see them in the tattered light. I stroke the .38 pistol. I wait, I wait, second after second, listening for the police, praying to be saved. This can't be true…

"He's over there," one of the shadows whispers, peering into my lair. "There he is."

I know it's time. I have to attack or die, it's that. I aim the .38 at the shadow and pull the trigger. A roar horrifies the night. The guy lets out a yell and crumbles to the floor. I aim the .38 at the other shadow, but it's scampering away, ducking out the door.

I hear sirens. The police coming to save me. They can't save me. I'm stalked by death and that is my life. Police will never come to save me, I can only save myself, or not. There's no such thing as protection, not for anybody.

My name will change, my address, my life. I only have one thing now; but it's better than all that:

I'm proud.

DEEP-FRIED HUMANS...

THE GRAPHITE SPIDER WAS hosting a monumental event for the new Emperor of the galaxy, The God Oren; Oren the Great. The super-carbon mass whose powerful image burst out in glorious light-waves to the countless worlds and domains that were now His—The God Oren, the awful being, fat on jellies and impossible treats. A God that, in a cloud-chair, had to be rolled by robots to the dinner table.

The graphite spider blinked its orbs at the Emperor. Hyper-electric tentacles splayed out from the Emperor's imperial armored multi-brain. A globe that sparkled royal red and royal blue and royal green and evil-white. The Lord Octopus of life and death. New Lord of the Galaxy.

"You have something special for me to try, Chef?" demanded the Emperor's jaws.

"Yes, My Lord." The graphite spider scrambled to produce his delicacies on the Emperor's table, blinking hatefully at the mechanicals scrambling to obey, to assure that everything was arranged just right, with all presentation in mind. "Majesty, my people not long ago received organized signals from a distant world in the Spiral Arms. We investigated and found there a very rare delicacy. I pray that you will enjoy it, My Lord."

Oren the Great made a loud fart. Its brain sparkled continuous electric colors. Its lethal worms of arms rolled life and death in their power. Murder and horror crackled out of every hole in the creature.

"The Spiral Arms is far away, Chef," said its maw. "We are so far impressed."

The graphite spider bowed and blinked lightbulb eyes. "A delicacy, Your Majesty—a treat that fried—that fried in a very special oil is quite rich in flavor and, I pray you find—delicious."

A mechanical worm of arm lifted one of the treats from the table—a fried-to-crisp man, plumply soaked in a sweet-and-sour sauce that dripped when lifted.

"Humans, these are called?"

"Yes, Majesty." The graphite spider made a clickering bow. "You are known as a great judge of galactic cuisine. I beg you to consider these exotic treats."

Oren the Great's million-sparkling eye danced over the graphite spider. "If I don't enjoy this treat, I may deem you unworthy, Chef. You should know what that would mean."

"No! I beg you, Majesty!" The graphite spider cringed. "We have gone to great lengths to present this delicacy to you!"

Oren farted. "I'm only joking, Chef. If I decide to kill you, there will be amusement involved—torture. Unimaginable torture, of course, for one who would wish to poison me with some exotic fare."

"No!"

"I'm only joking, Chef. Let me try one of your exotic delicacies." Oren's maw clattered open. It bit into the head of the fried man harvested from the far side of the galaxy. Oren the Great's skull crunched the treat, chewed like mesh, and sound modulated from its glittering mass.

"This is delicious, Chef." The million eyes glittered in satisfaction. "You must get me more of these."

"Of course, Excellency." The graphite spider's eyes blinked down. "It will be expensive, harvesting this product from so far away."

Oren the Great's maw sucked in and chewed the rest of the deep-fried human.

"What? Expensive? What expense is there to please God?"

"No expense, of course."

Oren farted. "Am I not God?"

"You are God," said the graphite spider.

The Emperor's worm-arm lifted another fried human from the table. It crunched it, sighing with pleasure. "Well done, Chef. These may now become one of Our favorite treats."

"There are many flavored oils they can be prepared in, Majesty. Human skull in Lavois oil and crunchy-nuts from Dara—a wonderful combination."

"Yes, I enjoy these human treats."

A deadly worm reached down to the table, this time a fried Earth female. Oren the Great crunched at the treat—the mechanical gullet suddenly paused…the hoped-for surprise.

"This one is juicer!"

"Yes, Sire. The females contain more fat and stored moisture."

"A distinctly different taste. I'll try another."

The graphite spider stood, eyes to the floor, blinking, as Oren the Great crunched down another Earth female. Its maw dripped greedily.

"Harvest these treats. See that it's done. They please my palate."

"I shall, Your Majesty."

"Well done, Chef. You have pleased Me, and so you will continue to live. Oh yes, these are addictive."

"I prayed you would enjoy them, My Lord."

"You said you discovered them by finding signals from them?"

"Yes, Majesty."

"These things were calling out, announcing their presence?"

"It seems so. We're still not certain why."

Oren farted. "A strange thing, when such tasty treats as these call out to us."

The graphite spider bowed. "Almost begging to be found and eaten."

Oren the Great took up another treat. "Fried like this they have a very salty and sweet taste. The skulls have a crispness that lends very well to the sweetness of the brain inside. Yes, I want more of these wonderful treats that call out to us."

The graphite spider stiffened to duty: "Yes, My Lord. My God."

ROADSIDE WILLIE'S BEASTS. . .

"RAJAH GOT OUT!"

Willie Jones stared at the broken cage. He stared round at the Nebraska countryside, the rolling hills of cropland and pasture, the miles of barbwire fence on either side of Highway 61. His caravan of exotic zoo animals hadn't planned on staying here beyond a night; not nearly enough business.

"Good God," Willie said. He continued to scan the quiet prairie as if he would be able to spot a Bengal tiger in the tall grass.

"No use, Boss," Avery said. "He's gone. He'll get the hell away from the open and find trees."

"What else will he find out there?"

"Food."

"Jesus. What do we do now?"

"Well, Hell, Boss. We gotta find him. Kill him if need be. A tiger loose in Cornville Nebraska?"

Willie gazed down the highway. His business had made a calculator of him—but this? "The county sheriff'll be here eventually, asking why we've not moved on."

"We'll just have to tell him."

"What? Oh, hell no! Then it'll be all about where's your animal permits, where's your licenses? I'd wind up in some local jail forever."

"That ain't nearly the worst that can happen, Boss."

"And so will you. For this they'll throw away the key on both of us. We'll lose this whole show, every animal, every truck and trailer, every tent and cage."

"That ain't the worst that could happen, Boss." Avery stared nervously at the prairie.

"Rajah's never been on his own. He was raised in a cage."

"He's a Bengal tiger, Boss. He's seven foot long and he weighs over 300 pounds. The biggest meat-eaters out here are coyotes and bobcats."

Willie stared off down the empty highway. "Look, Ave; if the law shows up, wondering why we're still camped here—illegally!—and starts wanting to ask questions and want documents—"

"I've seen you sweet-talk them before."

"Not for something like this."

He shuddered. This had always been a business that operated on the edge: a traveling roadside zoo that finds a good place to pitch camp, makes a lot of carney noise and brings the locals around to see exotic caged animals from the limits of the world. Only fifty cents and you will see a live alligator, a black widow spider, a Gila monster, a rattlesnake.

And here, folks, is the Tent of Terror! For only a quarter more from your pocketbook you will see the true demons of the earth: An African lion, an American Cougar! And the greatest, strongest, largest most dangerous and dominating land predator on this planet—

Rajah! A 300 pound Bengal tiger from the mysterious mists of ancient India! Don't gasp, my good people. The cage that holds Rajah is beyond his escape. He's well-fed, and being so has grown to a colossal size!

Roadside Willie's Beasts!

Willie stared away. "Jesus, Ave. I'm thinking we gotta move on."

"And leave Rajah loose out there? No, that can't happen. A tiger, Boss?"

"If it don't happen, we're gone; we're broke, we're lost, we're in jail."

"Boss, when he's found, they're going to know where he came from."

"Maybe not. Maybe he escaped from a private owner."

"What? Out here in Nebraska?"

"Some weird local who bought a tiger cub on the black market."

"Boss, what if he kills somebody?"

Willie's eyes darted around the pasture land and up and down the highway. He looked at his empire, the dilapidated trucks and outlandish painted trailers depicting wild beasts. A traveling zoo that local authorities always frowned at and watched closely.

"Maybe he'll just die out there," he muttered, half to himself.

"Boss, we gotta let the sheriff know—so they can warn the locals. Jesus, Boss, a full-grown tiger?"

"You want to be sitting in a jail out here, Ave? You want us to lose every damn thing we got?"

"What else? Just light out and not tell anybody anything?"

"The Iowa border's not 50 miles from here," Willie said. "The local sheriff probably don't even know we've passed this way yet."

"Oh God, Boss."

"That's my order, Ave. We get the hell out of this corn land as quick as we can."

"And leave a full-grown Bengal tiger loose out there?"

"We ain't got the time or money to get Raj back." Willie stared around one last time at the rolling land. "He could be miles away by now. Our biggest draw, and you let him escape."

"I told you that cage was getting dangerously rusty. I told you, Boss."

"Well, nothing we can do now but get out of here."

Farmer Ed Wilson stepped onto the porch. A cool summer night, the moon full and dime like.

What was wrong with the horses? They were raising heck out there in the corral, stomping, trampling, making a racket that echoed across the dark cornfield.

Ed stepped down off the porch and crossed over to the corral. He heard a strange huffing sound coming from the cedar break. He'd never heard a sound like that.

He knew something was wrong.

HELLO...

"ATTENTION," THE VOICE SAID quietly out of the speakers. At once it silenced the giant complex, and only the faint purring of computers could be heard. "People, the Mars explorer Hope has landed. All systems go!"

Cheers erupted. Technicians jumped up from their consoles and hugged and slapped high-fives. Dr. Bronson breathed a heavy sigh.

He grinned at the NASA team, skinny physicists and balding engineers, space geeks dancing, throwing up "Number One" fingers as if they were all quarterbacks after a touchdown pass. How wonderful this moment—how wonderful it is. To send a machine called Hope onto the very surface of Planet Mars.

"Okay, it's been done before, guys!" he called out. "Let's get focused now!"

But he couldn't stop grinning: their baby— the Martian probe Hope—the biting edge of technology, had landed and was now ready to crawl onto the red world.

Dr. Bronson trotted across the control room to Dr. Eldritch's station, which was monitoring radio signals to the robot probe waiting inconceivable miles away.

Eldritch grinned at him like a triumphant troll: "It all sounds pretty good." He offered his headphones to Dr. Bronson.

"No. It's getting strong signals?"

"It is."

"That's all I want to know. Here comes the real nail-bite: we got her down there, and we can talk to her. Now, can she roll down that ramp and start exploring?"

"She will. Relax, Stan. Is there any radio signal you want to test her with?"

Dr. Stanley Bronson grinned at Eldritch's mischievous face. "Send this: Dear people of Mars. Hello, Martians, it's us again. Sorry, but we're nosey. We won't mess up too much of your planet. Please forgive us."

Eldritch laughed, and when the radio signal was read out everybody in the complex broke into laughter and high fives.

"All right!" Bronson made a mock bow, to cheers and laughter. "We got her down safe and in one piece. Our baby seems to be in good shape; but we won't know until we take her out for a test drive."

Another round of cheers, then the NASA scientists and technicians returned eagerly to their stations. Robotic probes had landed and scoped the red world many times before, of course. But the thrill never lessened. The mind-boggling feat of sending a human machine to another world never failed to astound Dr. Bronson. Then telling it to wander, to explore, to scoop up dust beyond this very world and tell us what it is. Now there was tension, even fear in the complex. Eyes studied data; minds swam in the water with the millions of sharks that could destroy a venture like this. Pens were tapped on desks, throats swallowed, eyes blinked.

God…Oh God. The red world. Dr. Stanley Bronson knew what it was, had always known: a dead world, desolate and empty. He had never believed Mars could have life, or ever did have it. Our red sister was always barren. We can find water, but we won't find life.

It doesn't matter, he thought, staring with pride at his NASA team, bent intensely over their computer screens, aching to see Hope come onto the stage and behold the alien world.

A dead world.

No, I can't say that, Bronson thought. In order to be dead you had to once have been alive.

He didn't believe that Mars, or any planets or moons in this solar system—besides Earth—were ever alive. It was only man's longing that questioned facts and evidence. The desire by some scientists to appear on the Discovery Channel and cash in on the old Life-On-Mars fantasy.

The science of Mars exploration was, Bronson felt, too compromised by the great poison of human nature, which infected great scientists and everyone else: believing something to be true because you Want it to be true.

Please find evidence of life on Mars, Hope. How many of my beloved colleagues are saying that in their minds—or praying that—at this moment?

Dr. Bronson had never believed there was life on Mars. But the scarlet dot in the sky had captured him anyway. And now his adorably cute little graphite spider-child was about to take her first robot steps onto its startling surface. My child—Hope—entering a dead world, seeing what was never seen before.

Many brilliant people believe nonsense, he knew. Sir Arthur Conan Doyle believed in fairies. Great astronomers saw canals and constructions and carved faces on Mars. In my lifetime people worried about Martians attacking Planet Earth…yet everything we find out there is dead, and will be for the time being.

"Stan." Dr. Eldritch startled him from behind. "We're getting radio signals from Hope."

"Good. Okay, let's get her down the ramp and begin—"

"Stan, there's something." Eldritch gave him a strange look.

"Oh, damn it. What's wrong?"

"Nothing. Nothing's wrong." Eldritch shook his mystified eyes. "It's…strange."

"What? Are we having communication problems?"

Eldritch's voice dropped to a whisper: "Stan, we got some initial radio interference. It had to be from Earth. It's cleared up now."

"What do you mean?"

"Radio signals from Earth. Not the rover."

Bronson stared at him. "That's not possible. What are you talking about?"

"Come over here."

Bronson followed him to the console and immediately donned a set of headphones.

"This is the first signal we got from the rover," Eldritch said.

He played the recorded signal back. Bronson heard a series of strange, disjointed beeps and short buzzes, then silence.

He took off the headphones. "What is it? Don't tell me our radio communication is screwing up. Please don't tell me that."

"No, it's working to perfection," Eldritch said.

"Thank God. So this was just initial interference?"

"I thought so—at first," Eldritch said.

"What?"

Dr. Eldritch gave him a very strange look. "Were you in the Boy Scouts, Stan?"

Bronson scowled. "No. The Boy Scouts?"

"I had to earn a merit badge, and I chose to memorize Morse Code," Eldritch said. "That's why this initial radio signal had to have come from Earth."

"You know as well as I do that that's impossible," Bronson said. "Some electro-magnetic surge interfered with our radio contact for a few seconds. It might have sounded like Morse Code or something. But we have it back, right?"

"Yes. We've got good radio contact. Everything's perfect; she should be able to roll out there and start sending us information."

"All right. That's all that matters."

Eldritch gave him a look.

"What the hell's the matter?"

"Stan…that radio signal was Morse Code."

"Oh, come on. It couldn't have come from Earth."

"If it couldn't have come from Earth, then it came from Mars."

"Morse Code wasn't programmed into the rover."

"I know that. But here it is."

"Right…so what's the message?"

"In Morse Code, the message is this: Thank you for warning us. We forgive you."

DAWN...

"I T'LL HURT, WON'T IT?" the boy asked.

He could maybe have been my last son, she thought. In another world. A boy too young to have to die like this.

Helena leaned over and spat on the stone floor of the dungeon. Best not to think that; to not know his name, or know that he would die in the morning.

"Will it hurt, Mother?" The boy was trying to keep his courage. He was trying to hold onto what they had said to him: Die with courage; die with honor.

"I'm not your mother."

"Will it hurt?"

"It will," she said. "But not for long."

"Then what?"

Helena shrugged. "Then we'll know what no other living thing knows. Or not."

It was quiet for awhile. The boy stared down at the stone floor that was almost lost in the dark.

Helena spat again, in anger, surprised she could still make it in her mouth. She should be deeply afraid; but she was only tired. Strange how it comforted her that at this time, in this place, she was only tired and not afraid. But the boy shouldn't have to die like this in the fruiting of life.

"I believe in God," the boy muttered at the stone floor. "Do you?"

"I used to," the old woman said. "I believed in many things. I believed in my two sons who were shot by them. I believed in my husband who was shot by them. I don't know what I believe now. What I believe doesn't matter."

"That's why you went out to fight them."

She looked at him, then away. Best not to look at him. "Why did you go out to fight them?"

"They're the enemy."

"Yes, the enemy." Helena stared at the steel door held in stone walls that went up into the dark. It was so dark she could see only a few of the others, some already dead. Shadows in shadows. The living dead holding fear and despair in their laps and arms.

The boy began to cry. "Before they came I—there was a girl, Sondra. I was going to ask her to be my wife."

Helena almost said that it was a pretty name, Sondra. But best not. "Then they came and you went out to fight them. What became of the girl?"

"I don't know."

"Well, we fought them. They can have everything but that."

"I believe I'll see Sondra in Heaven," the boy said. "When it's her time. And you'll see your husband and your sons there. Don't you believe?"

"Yes, I believe," she lied. "But we can talk about that to God. Now it's best not to speak. Just think of her and make peace with life. It never lasts for anything."

The boy covered his eyes and began sobbing. All around them dark; the smell of mildew and hay and sweat of these doomed shadows that smelled like piss. She thought of how terrible is the stink of war—the unending stink of it, and how human beings could march so proudly into the stinking mess.

I did. I marched into it with all the hate in the world. The old woman who fights.

And seeing just an old woman, one day an enemy turned his back and Helena shot him in the head. She was not blameless. Many of these shadows in the dark with her—most—were not blameless, and should be dead. Helena had seen it on both sides, what mindless hate is.

But not the boy. He seemed too young to deserve this, to have seen so much that hate took him over.

Helena stared into the dark. She had killed more than one of them. She had killed many of them, as only a sad old harmless widow could:

But this waiting for death. The boy couldn't deserve it. Death riding dawn across the earth. This was merciless death for a boy so young. Making him sit in this stinking tomb until dawn sends light through that steel window up there and then it's his time.

In another world he would be taking Sondra into his arms, and they would know young love and young joy. They would have seen the faces of children in the warm sun.

Helena had seen them—long ago. So precious they made her want to believe. But if she were to meet her husband in Heaven, her sons, dead before their time, would they be as precious as what is lost forever?

Now the world was a dungeon. Helena knew some of the doomed shadows were counting seconds on their dark fingers, staring at the window of steel that stood too high to reach up the wet stone wall where the sun would come and make the beginning of the last day.

"I'm sorry to talk," the boy finally blurted out. "I'm afraid. And I'm getting more afraid. I am afraid. Please talk to me."

"About what?"

"About—how it will be."

"I don't know," she said. "I've never been executed."

"Mother—Ma'am…please. I'm afraid."

"You will show great courage when the time comes. You will make me very proud of you, and you will be known as a great hero."

"But then…"

"Then God will welcome you into Heaven. And one day Sondra will come to you, more beautiful than you can imagine."

"That is what will happen?"

"I'm sure of it. I'll see my husband and my children, and you'll see Sondra."

The boy shuddered at the dark stone floor. "I'm scared. I'm—"

Helena stared into the dark. This was no way for a boy like this to die. Look, God, if You are truly there, then I give up my only prayer. Do not forgive me for killing so many of the enemy, send me to hell if You have to. I would have killed more. You know why I did what I did, or You're not God. Only forgive the boy, and let him get out of this dark. Only let the boy out of this hell.

"I want to see Sondra again!" the boy said. "That's all I want."

"You will see her again," Helena said. "Close your eyes and think about her. You'll be wandering about Heaven, and one day she'll appear to you, more beautiful than you could have imagined."

"I believe in God," said the boy. "This can't be all there is—to die. There has to be more than just to live and die."

"You're very wise for your age." Helena smiled at the dark rock tomb that stank of her comrades' piss-sweat. The boy was probably not wise, but she wanted to give him some comfort before dawn crawled into the steel-barred window.

Helena didn't know why. It didn't matter if she gave him hope or not. For the boy who shouldn't die like this, it might as well be hope.

"I believe in God," the boy said. His eyes were now glancing up at the dark window of bars.

(How close is the dawn?)

She smiled at the stone floor. "For you there will be a little pain, but not much. Then it'll be over. You'll find yourself standing before God and then you'll march into Heaven as you marched against the enemy. And one day Sondra will come to you."

"And you'll be there with me," the boy said. "With your husband and your sons in Heaven."

"That is how it will be. That's what I believe," she lied. "You and Sondra couldn't be together here on this world, because God meant for you to be together in Heaven."

"Yes! I believe that! I believe that."

"That is what will happen in the morning." Helena stared into the dark. She remembered her husband, her sons, gone into the dark. Everything goes there. But the boy shouldn't have to go so young; not like this, smells and darkness and waiting.

I remember seeing dawn bloom over the farm, before they came. My sons strong lifting hay and my husband laughing around his pipe. The dawn making joy on his face. I remember how dawn was before they came.

"I'm afraid," the boy whispered. "I'm so afraid."

"God will be kind. He will forgive. You'll only go to a better place. And then Sondra will come to you."

"I'm...sorry," the boy said. "Oh, God!"

The shadows in this crypt stirred suddenly. Red dawn came alive. Shadows scrambled off the stone floor, looking at the window, and the first red of dawn. A steel clanking march was the enemy coming down stone steps, marching down to perform the executions. It was the time—the crunching, steel-marching time.

"We're going to die!" the boy said.

Helena stared up at the faint red sunlight. "Everyone dies."

"But...what you say is true? I'll see Sondra in Heaven?"

Helena smiled at him, the boy who shouldn't have to die like this.

"I know it's true," she lied.

The End...